Celia Rees writes: I am interested in the way that the past underlies the present; how perfectly ordinary places, otherwise hardly worth a second glance, are shadowed by sinister events from the past. Many of our ancient cities host ghost walks which invite us to visit such places and it was on just such a walk that I had the idea for this series. I found myself thinking: What if there were two cities? The one we live in – and one that ghosts inhabit. What if at certain times of the year and in certain places, the barriers between the two worlds grow thin, making it possible to move from one to the other? And if ghosts lived there, why not others? Creatures we know from myth and legend, creatures so powerful that even the ghosts fear them? Just a story? Maybe. But on a recent visit to that city, I found that several of the ghost walk routes had been abandoned, because of poltergeist activity . . .

Celia Rees has written many books for children and teenagers and enjoys writing in different genres. She hopes what interests her will interest other people, be it ghosts, vampires, UFOs or witch trials. Her latest books, *Truth or Dare* and *Witch Child*, have been published to critical acclaim.

Other titles available from Hodder Children's Books:

The Brugan
Dead Edward
Stephen Moore

Daughter of Storms
The Dark Caller
Keepers of Light
Mirror Mirror 1: Breaking Through
Mirror Mirror 2: Running Free
Mirror Mirror 3: Testing Limits
Louise Cooper

Owl Light
Night People
Alien Dawn
Maggie Pearson

Power to Burn
Anna Fienberg

The Lammas Field
Catherine Fisher

The Law of the Wolf Tower
Queen of the Wolves
Tanith Lee

The Boxes
William Sleator

The Host Rides Out

CELIA REES

Hodder
Children's
Books

a division of Hodder Headline Limited

First published as separate volumes:
T is for Terror and *S is for Shudder* in 1998
by Hodder Children's Books

This bind-up edition published in 2002
by Hodder Children's Books Limited

10 9 8 7 6 5 4 3 2

A Catalogue record for this book
is available from the British Library

ISBN 0 340 81802 6

Typeset by Hewer Text Ltd, Edinburgh
Printed and bound in Great Britain by
Clays Ltd, St Ives plc

Hodder Children's Books
A Division of Hodder Headline Limited
338 Euston Road
London NW1 3BH

Easter

The Host Rides Out

All through the city and its suburbs, the past lies behind the present and ghosts shadow the living. There are threshold zones, borderlines, and places where the laws of time and space falter. Strange things can happen, the barriers between the worlds grow thin and it is possible, just possible, to move from one world to another . . . And when a psychic storm rages, Davey Williams risks his own life to save his friends – and faces a final confrontation with an old, malicious enemy: the Lady . . .

Come away, O human child!
To the waters and the wild
With a faery, hand in hand,
For the world's more full of weeping than
you can understand.

W.B. Yeats 'The Stolen Child'

And if any gaze on our rushing band,
We come between him and the deed of his hand,
We come between him and the hope of his heart.

W.B. Yeats 'The Hosting of the Sidhe'

'Hey, Davey, look at this.'

Davey's sister Kate held up the local paper for him to see.

Relics Return to Cathedral
'little short of miraculous'

Relics recently discovered in the old part of the city, and thought to be those of St Wulfric, founder of the Cathedral of St John the Baptist, are to be returned to their former resting-place after a period of more than four hundred years.

Provost Michael Campion told our reporter that the find was 'little short of the miraculous' and that there are plans afoot to restore the original shrine situated in the chapel that still bears the saint's name.

Davey Williams scanned the article. He had been there when the saint's relics had been rediscovered. He and Kate, along with their cousins, Tom and Elinor, had played a vital part in getting them restored to their rightful place. He smiled to himself as he read. Although he knew all about this, it was still satisfying to see it in print. He was just about to give the paper back to his sister when his attention was caught by an article on the opposite page.

Ghostly Goings-on

Reports of ghostly goings-on have been pouring in from all over the city: everything from mystery monks moving past the cathedral in ghostly procession, to horsemen haunting Hollow Lane.

Hi-tech Chaos

Even modern offices are not immune. Firms situated off Market Square have reported hi-tech chaos: unaccountable computer malfunctions, mystery faxes and phantom photocopies.

Shiver Corner

At one of the city's oldest pubs, the Dyer's Arms on Harrow Lane, landlady Mrs Brenda Meakin tells of strange noises coming up from the cellar. 'Some nights it sounds like all hell's broken loose,' she says. Many a morning, Norman the landlord finds barrels moved, crates overturned, coolers and pumps turned off. Alsatian guard dog, Prince, normally known for his fierceness, refuses to go down there at all!

Other residents of Harrow Lane have reported a

phantom horseman and eerie hoof beats at the dead of night. Running footsteps have also been heard along nearby Johnswell Passage. Such experiences are forcing residents to consider renaming the area 'Shiver Corner'.

Apparitions

The local tourist board might have seen this as an extra draw in a city famous for its ghost tours, but their offices on Butcher Row have also been hit: brochures and leaflets misplaced, computer files erased. Ghosts have been glimpsed here at regular intervals, dating back to the time when the building was an inn, *The Seven Dials*. Mrs Diane Jarvis, manageress of the Rosebud Café next door, also reports disturbances: cutlery hurled, glass and crockery broken.

Ghost-hunters Called In

Things have got so bad that local people have called in a team of ghost-hunters. Mrs Sylvia Craggs, psychic, medium and Chairperson of SIPPAP, The Society for the Investigation of Psychic, Paranormal and Associated Phenomena, prefers the term 'paranormal investigators'. She goes on to say: 'The current outbreak may be linked to recent redevelopment in and around the old part of the city. We are taking it very seriously and I can confirm that we have been called upon to look into it.'

Davey studied the article carefully before handing the paper over to Kate. As she read down the page, her expression stayed serious and thoughtful. The reporter's jokey tone left her cold. She knew, as Davey did, that there was another city, a ghost city, existing parallel to their own. Something very serious must be going on there for it to show itself like this. She looked across at her brother. The inn of *The Seven Dials* was home to a ghost crew she and Davey knew well. Polly, Elizabeth and Govan lived there with their captain, the highwayman, Jack Cade. Kate read the part about ghost-hunters again. She did not like the sound of that. It could mean trouble for their ghost friends.

'Maybe we could go into town early,' Davey suggested. 'Check it out. I've got a feeling . . .'

Kate nodded. There was no need for him to say more. There had been a time when she had dismissed Davey's 'feelings', his intuitions and premonitions, as fantasy, laughed at them even. Not now. They had been through too much for that.

'If we went in straight away,' Davey went on, 'we could have a scout round before we have to meet Tom and Ellie. What do you think?'

Tom and Elinor, their twin cousins, were coming to

stay for a combination of the May Day weekend and Kate's birthday. Their bus was not due in until 6:30, which left plenty of time . . .

Davey stood up. 'Let's go, then. Have a nose about. Find out what's happening.'

Kate and Davey took the bus. They had to get out at the terminus in the new part of the city. Open tour buses were the only ones allowed into the Old Town.

They crossed the river and made their way up Fore Street to the cathedral and Market Square. As they passed the Market Cross, Davey kept an eye out for the board advertising Haunts Ghost Tours. Davey always looked out for it. It reminded him of the tour they had gone on last midsummer; their first visit to the hidden city. He jogged Kate's arm. The Haunts Tours board wasn't there any more. Neither were any of the others. All the ghost tour notices had been removed.

To Davey this seemed ominous, but Kate thought that there was probably some simple explanation.

'Let's ask her.' She pointed to a familiar figure: Louise, their Haunts Tours guide from last midsummer. 'She ought to know.'

Louise was lounging next to a City Walks hoarding and no longer sported flowing black gothic clothes. Her ample form was squeezed into a skirt and blazer and, instead of carrying a staff with a plastic skull on the top of it, she wore a straw boater as her badge of office.

'Hi,' Kate said. 'You used to do Haunts Tours, didn't you? We went on one last year. It was really good. We wanted to go again, now the nights are getting lighter, but there's no sign out. What's happened?'

'Haunts has gone out of business,' Louise replied. 'Temporarily, so they say, but I don't know so much. Tell you one thing,' she gave a slight shudder, 'I won't be working for them again.'

'Oh, why's that?'

'Got a bit too *real* for me,' the older girl shivered again, despite the warmth of the day. 'Especially in the underground city. You remember down there?'

Kate nodded. The heart of the Haunts Tour was a visit to sad remnants of streets and dwellings, now built over and forgotten. They lay under the present city levels. Kate remembered them well. Even now, she could recall the damp stone smell.

'Well, it was always kind of atmospheric,' Louise looked nostalgic. 'I didn't mind it then. It was a good laugh, winding up the punters, but it began to get really creepy. All sorts of people began seeing things and hearing things – you didn't have to be psychic – and then things started happening.'

'What kinds of things?'

'All kinds. Sudden changes in temperature, objects appearing and disappearing, lights going on and off for no reason. Rocks falling. The door jamming. Freaked me out that did – I thought we were locked in. Management

6

said it was damp getting in, all that building work making it unstable. Whatever the reason, it was downright dangerous. And some of the noises . . .' she hugged her arms to her, violet blue eyes wide with remembered terror, '. . . enough to chill the blood.'

'What kind of noises?'

'Screaming, shouting, crying, sounded like a barrel-load of banshees. Management said it was "amplified traffic noise".' Louise snorted her contempt. 'They have *got* to be joking! It was so bad in the end that I handed in my notice.' She pushed back her boater. 'Thought I'd try my hand at straight tours instead.' She peered over their shoulders at a group of advancing tourists. 'And I think I've got customers, so you'll have to excuse me. Like I said,' she added, as she got out her book of tickets. 'I wouldn't ever work for Haunts again.'

2

Kate and Davey went across the square and on into the oldest part of the city, threading their way through the picturesque warren of streets, following the signs to the Tourist Information Office. They were following roughly the same route as they had taken last year on the Haunts Ghost Tour. Davey stopped every now and again to test the atmosphere. He remembered getting goosebumps just about here last midsummer. He'd had this feeling that someone was following them; he'd kept thinking he heard a soft footfall and light whispered laughter. He turned again, knowing now that it had been Elizabeth, but this time he felt nothing.

His psychic sense had developed a lot since then. More importantly, he had learned to trust it, to believe in his premonitions, his sudden insights and powerful intuitions. He had learnt not to deny that he had them and not to fight them. He knew how to open himself up and let the feelings flow through him. He did that now but again felt nothing. No indication of any kind of presence, of Elizabeth or anybody else. After what he'd read in the newspapers, after what Louise had just said, he had thought to pick up a world in tumult. Maybe his psychic sense had deserted him?

On the other hand, maybe the ghosts had left this part of the city. Been forced out by the ghost-hunters. He looked around, but his eyes were unseeing, and into his mind came an image of a city torn by war. One area full of frantic activity, while another lay deserted and empty. He was suddenly sure that the same thing was happening here. They were in a battle zone, walking through a war they could not see, and at the centre of it stood *The Seven Dials*.

Davey stood for a moment in front of the large black-and-white building on Butcher's Row where the inn had once been. It was now the Tourist Information Office. He looked up, his head cocked to one side, hoping to hear the ghost of a laugh, see the flicker of a face in the diamond panes. But there was nothing. He glanced towards the café next door, the one that had been mentioned in the newspaper report. He had been there with Elizabeth. Davey thought of her now; visualised the two of them together. If she was around, then surely thinking about that would bring her out? But the air was neutral around him. He felt nothing.

Davey followed Kate into the Tourist Information Office. The large room was a centre of activity. It was a Saturday at the end of April so there were plenty of tourists there, leafing through the brochures, asking about accommodation. Kate and Davey paused by the door. Davey looked round and then gave a slight shake of the head; still negative. A little red light winked from a small white metal box fixed in a corner between the wall and the ceiling. Davey wondered fleetingly what its function might be, then turned away with a shrug. It was probably some kind of miniature closed circuit video camera, or 'electronic eye' security system.

Kate showed the newspaper article to the woman behind the desk and asked if she knew anything about it. Kate said she was doing a project, always a favourite way of getting adult co-operation. Not this time, though. The woman didn't seem to want to talk. She said they were too busy, to come back another day.

'What shall we do now?' Kate asked as they got outside.

Davey looked round the courtyard. It was not exactly like it was when the place was *The Seven Dials*. The main features were the same: the cobbled floor, the gallery running round, the half-timbering. But the age-silvered wood and pale brown plaster had been given a smart coat of black and white. Tables from the whole-food café in the corner spilled over half the cobbles. Small shop units had been set up round the sides. People were milling everywhere. There was no possibility of making any contact. The site had about as much atmosphere as a supermarket.

'Hello, you two,' a voice said behind him. 'What are you doing here?'

Davey turned to see Dr Jones, the young archaeologist from the City Museum, smiling down over a brown paper sack of shopping. For a moment Davey wondered what she was doing here herself, then he remembered that she lived in a flat above the Tourist Information Office.

'We're, er . . .'

'Doing a project,' Kate put in, nodding towards the Tourist Board door.

'Together? But aren't you in different years?'

'Yes. It's Davey's project. I'm giving him a hand.'

Mari Jones shifted the bag to her other arm. 'What's it about? Maybe I can help.'

'I don't think so,' Kate said quickly.

'Yes,' Davey said at the same time.

'Well, make up your minds,' Mari Jones flicked her dark red hair back and looked down at them, her greeny-brown eyes laughing and quizzical. She shifted the weight of her bag again. 'Tell you what? Why don't you come upstairs with me? I can dump this lot and then we can have a cup of tea and you can tell me all about it.'

Dr Jones's flat was one big room. Thick beams ran through uneven whitewashed walls and exposed rafters spanned the wide oak-planked floors. The sparse furnishings had been carefully chosen to allow the beauty of the old building to show through.

'Did you see in the paper?' Mari Jones came from the kitchen area carrying a tray of tea. 'The relics are back in the cathedral.'

Davey nodded. He and Kate had been there at the Easter rescue dig when the bones of the saint had been found. After that, they had been involved in a struggle to save them from those, both living and dead, who had been bent on stealing them for their own evil purposes. Dr Jones had played her own part in keeping the relics safe from harm.

'How did you convince the cathedral authorities that the bones belonged to St Wulfric?' Kate asked.

'Ultimately we can't be absolutely certain that they do belong to him, although the carbon dating puts them mid-seventh century, which fits with the historical record. This is the really interesting thing, the clincher if you like.' She leaned forward to pour the tea. 'You remember Dr Monckton?'

The two children nodded. They took their cups from her silently. The sinister archivist had been in league with the most evil presences in the ghost city. The forces he had almost succeeded in unleashing had been absolutely terrifying. How could they forget?

'Well,' the archaeologist sipped her tea and continued, 'you know those papers he was working on?' They nodded again. The papers had come from the Judge's house. 'Among them was an inventory from the Benedictine Priory. Those monastic houses were huge, like small cities, with highly organised bureaucracies. Periodically they would list all their assets: the things they owned. Relics were highly valued, and among the barrels of this and sacks of that was a description of the relics, right down to the piece missing out of the skull. Now the bones might or might not be those of St Wulfric,' she spread her hands, 'for all we know he might not even have existed, but they *are* the relics that the monks reverenced; the inventory proves it. So there you have it. Now,' she sat back, arms folded, 'what are you doing here?'

'We – we,' Kate started.

She was unsure what to say, but Davey looked up and met the archaeologist's sharp gaze. He hesitated for a moment and then reached into his pocket and fished out the page from the newspaper.

'We came because we saw this,' he said as he handed over the crumpled paper.

Mari Jones smoothed the creases out on her knee and began to scan the article on 'Ghostly Goings-on'.

'I see,' she said, when she had finished reading. She folded the paper carefully before returning it to Davey.

'We just wondered . . .' began Davey. 'Well, what we wondered was . . . Oh, thanks . . .'

Davey took the paper from her and then made a fuss of re-folding it and putting it in his pocket. He could not think what to say.

'You live here,' Kate put in. 'Maybe you could tell us what's been happening. I mean, why were the ghost-hunters brought in?'

Mari Jones didn't answer straight away. She looked at the two of them sitting side by side on the sofa. They were very different. One fair, one dark; one tall and willowy, the other short and thick-set; but they both had the same

13

intense look on their faces, the same level of interest in their eyes. There was something strange about them, she'd felt it before – especially the boy, Davey.

'Well,' she leaned forward, 'it's pretty much as you read there. There was a certain amount of disturbance down-stairs, probably a glitch in the electrical systems, but someone mentioned poltergeists. Then the cleaners start seeing things, sensing presences. One of them is psychic, apparently, and she pronounced the spirits who live here to be "deeply unhappy". Next thing you know, they've brought in these people. I think it's some kind of publicity stunt, personally. Get people into this place and boost interest in the city . . .'

'What people?' Davey asked. 'Who are they exactly?'

'There were two of them, a man and a woman.'

'What did they do?'

'Some kind of exorcism, I should imagine. I wasn't there, so I'm not sure. The woman called it "a Banish-ing", the man said it was "a Cleansing".'

'How do you know, if you weren't there?' Kate asked.

'Because they offered to do the same thing up here. Perform the same ceremony or whatever. Odd couple. She seemed all right, a bit cold and stand-offish – more I don't know, old-fashioned, like a medium or something. Talked about "interceding with the spirits". He was different. All high-tech. Brought in a shed-load of equip-ment. Even left a little gizmo down there to keep it clear. I wasn't sure about him.' She shook her head. 'I reckon he

14

was a bit of a con artist. Anyway, I didn't want him messing about up here.' She looked round the beautiful tranquil room with the afternoon sun slanting through diamond panes. 'This is an old building. I chose to live here because of it. If it has ghosts, I'd consider that a plus.' She shrugged. 'They are welcome to stay.'

'So you believe in them?' Davey looked at her. 'Ghosts, I mean.'

'I wouldn't go quite that far.' She laughed, then added, 'But in my line of work we come across some strange things.' She leaned forward, suddenly serious. 'Oh, you won't find them written up in journals and papers, but occasionally things happen that can't be explained in any ordinary way.' She stood up and went over to a bureau, opened the top drawer and took something out. 'Take these, for example. You know the Johnswell, where I met you once – I told you we did a dig there?' They both nodded. 'Well, during the dig, I found these.' She held out the objects for them to see. A football medal and a fifty pence piece. Davey and Kate did not look at each other. 'Nothing strange about that, you might say, except they were found with objects from the seventeenth century. Even then,' she began to pace up and down, the objects clasped in her hand, 'such finds could be put down to modern contamination of the site, thrown in by a passer-by, fallen out of someone's pocket. Except, except,' she held them tighter now, 'this particular fifty pence piece was not in circulation at the time it was found, and this

15

particular player was not even in the league, let alone the England team. Strange, eh?'

Davey and Kate nodded and looked away. They had seen the objects before. They had thrown them into the Johnswell themselves.

'It's an anomaly,' Mari Jones added, as she continued to pace the room. 'There is no rational explanation. I come across examples all the time. Like I said, you won't find it reported in academic papers, but some of my colleagues find dowsing, someone holding a couple of sticks, far more reliable for locating sites than geophysics. There are other things, too.' She stopped her pacing and stood still in the centre of the room. 'Sometimes, when I've been out on site somewhere remote, up on the downs, say, or the high moorland, and it's late in the evening, or early on a misty morning, and there's no one else around, then I've felt it. I've never actually *seen* anything, but it's hard not to feel the presence of all the people who've lived, and worked, and worshipped, and died there. Perhaps over thousands of years.' She gave a slight shiver. 'I don't know if that's what people mean by ghosts, but if it is, then, yes,' she turned to them with a smile, 'I guess I do believe, and I don't think that anybody should interfere with them.'

'Like those people, you mean? The couple who came to see you?'

'Yes, Davey, like them.'

'I still don't really understand what they actually do,' Kate said.

16

'Hang on a minute.' Mari Jones went back to the bureau from which she had taken the finds and came back with a card. 'Here. They gave me this.'

She handed the card to Kate. It read:

Society for the Investigation of Psychic,
Paranormal and Associated Phenomena
Chairperson: Mrs Sylvia Craggs
Psychic Consultant: Eugene Hutton FIPR
13 Fiddler's Court
Old Town

'If you want to know more about what they do,' Mari Jones said, 'I suggest you go and see them.'

3

Before they went to the Society's offices in Fiddler's Court, Davey suggested a quick detour. He wanted to go to Keeper's Stairs, to see if there was still a way into the underground city. If there was, he explained to Kate, then they could go to the Room of Ceremonies and use the mirror to get through to see what was really happening.

Kate was not keen on this idea at all, but she knew how hard it was to deflect Davey once he was set on something. If she did not go with him, he was likely to go on his own, and Kate hated to imagine the consequences of that. It was safer for her to go along with him and pray that they could not get in.

Kate's prayers were answered. Not only was the door locked, but it was secured with a hefty padlock. Davey rattled this a couple of times and turned away disappointed. He was desperate now to know how things were within the ghost city. The disquiet he had felt before had been growing all the time that Dr Jones had been talking. It was turning now into a fever of frustration.

'Never mind, Davey.' Kate flicked the card Dr Jones had given to her. 'Let's go and find out what this lot are up to.'

★　　★　　★

The Society for the Investigation of Psychic, Paranormal and Associated Phenomena – SIPPAP for short – and formerly known as just the Society – had occupied the same premises in Fiddler's Court for over a century. The Society had been set up in 1887 by a Doctor Aston, a medical doctor who considered himself to be both a scientist and a philosopher. His stated aim was to 'examine in a scientific spirit those phenomena, both real and supposed, which defy rational explanation'. He had quickly attracted other like-minded persons to him and the Society had grown to become one of the country's foremost organisations dedicated to the investigation of matters related to the after-life, mediumship and the paranormal. They had investigated everything from full-scale hauntings to table-rapping, and had an almost unrivalled collection of case histories. The Society had declined in recent years, both in membership and reputation, to become a rather old-fashioned, sleepy organisation, its work largely ignored and forgotten, carried on by a few stalwarts like Mrs Sylvia Craggs.

Not any more. Recently the Society had experienced a transformation, both in membership and fortune. It now had its own magazine and website. Under the guidance of Mr Eugene Hutton, Psychic Consultant, SIPPAP investigated a host of unexplained phenomena, from UFOs to crop circles, the perfect organisation for the twenty-first century.

Kate and Davey knew none of this as they stood in

front of the tall grey stone town house set back from the street behind freshly painted black iron railings. Wide stone steps led up to a large front door with a polished brass knocker in the shape of a lion's head. Kate and Davey mounted the steps and stood, undecided about what to do next. The knocker was seldom used, the hinge was stiff with the white residue of brass polish. Kate looked round for some kind of bell or buzzer and saw a row of them set into the wall. She pushed the button next to the initials: SIPPAP. The Society no longer took up the whole building. The offices were on the upper two floors.

A squawk from a small loudspeaker made Kate jump.

She pressed another button, and stood on tiptoe, speaking into the little grille.

'Hello? Is that the Society?' She waited a second and then carried on. 'We'd like to come up and talk to you. We want to know more about what you do.'

There was no voice reply, but a buzzer sounded and the lock clicked back. Davey reached down and turned the brass handle.

They pushed the door back, leaving it slightly ajar, and walked into a wide hall with grey polished stone-flagged floors. Heavy cream-painted doors led off right and left, but these were firmly shut. Davey and Kate walked on towards a mahogany banistered staircase twisting away to the upper storeys. Davey was suddenly reminded of Derry House. He'd gone in there at Hallowe'en and the place had terrified him. His footsteps faltered and he half wanted to run, but he made himself go on. This was not the same at all, he told himself. Kate was with him, for one thing, and they were here in broad daylight. This was not some dark, dusty, deserted, paper-peeling, rat-infested, crumbling dump. This building was used all the time. There was a vase of fresh flowers and a pile of mail stacked on the table under the stairs. All the doors had little brass plaques showing the names of the companies. The hall smelt nice and fresh, of scent from the flowers and lavender floor polish, not all dank and damp.

'I put them there myself.' A voice from just above their heads made them start. 'Lilies. My favourites. Such a divine smell. Some don't like it, of course. Reminds them of funerals.'

Kate and Davey looked up to see a woman leaning over the curving banister. She was tall and thin and stern-looking, with strong features and a prominent high-bridged hawk-like nose. She was middle-aged, even older, but wore her hair long, swept back from her forehead. Her black hair showed no grey, apart from one streak of white at the front on the right hand side. Her eyes were darker than Davey's, almost black; they watched him now from under hooded lids.

'I never forget a face,' Mrs Craggs said and smiled, showing prominent ivory-coloured teeth.

Davey knew her, too. She had been in the Rosebud Café when Elizabeth had shown him how to haunt.

Elizabeth had warned him to be careful of her. The woman was a medium and she had seen them . . .

Davey began to back away, but he was a fraction too late. The big front door shut with a loud click as a long arm shot out and strong fingers gripped him firmly by the wrist.

4

'Just checking for a pulse,' the woman said and then released him. 'You'd better come up,' she added, jerking her head towards the floor above.

She turned with a swirl of her floral skirt and Kate and Davey followed her up the stairs to the Society's offices.

'Like I said, I never forget a face,' her hooded black eyes brooded on Davey. 'Now who are you? And what do you want? And don't lie to me,' she shook her ringed forefinger at him. 'I'll know in an instant.'

'I – I'm,' Davey cleared his throat and started again. 'My name is Davey Williams and this is my sister Kate.'

'Sylvia Craggs,' the woman introduced herself. 'Sit down, sit down.' She waved towards two hardback chairs covered in boxes. 'Shift that rubbish. That's right. Now what can I do for you?' She asked again when they were seated.

'We've come to see you because we read about this—' Davey took out the newspaper story and spread it out. 'We know, about the ghosts, you see, particularly the ones at *The Seven* Dials, the Tourist Information Office as it is now. We want to know what's going on, if – if they're safe, and—'

23

'Wait! Wait!' She held up her hand and moved to a large untidy desk. 'Get rid of these for me, there's a good lad.' She picked up a heap of papers and handed them to Davey. 'Box by your feet. That'll do. Now, how did you get into this?' Sitting down, she picked up a pencil, pushed a small portable typewriter out of the way, and reached for a yellow legal notepad. 'I think you'd better start at the beginning, don't you?'

Davey did as he was told. He thought back and told her about all the things that had happened to them since last midsummer. Starting from when they first went through the portal in the underground city, to the battle for the relics in the basement of the museum. Kate listened while he spoke, occasionally adding a detail or two to back him up, but he seemed to be getting on fine. Her attention soon wandered to the room itself.

The room was strange, intriguing. She had not expected to see computers and fax machines for one thing. She looked above the level of office clutter to the portraits of past presidents that lined the oak-panelled walls. Dark paintings of austere Victorians ranging up to modern photographs of men in lounge suits: doctors, scientists, churchmen and psychics, ghost-watchers all, looked down with penetrating eyes. In between them, the walls were hung with photographs of the most haunted places in Britain: gaunt ruins etched against open skies; hulking castles brooding at the end of tree-lined avenues; gloomy rectories with steeply-pitched gables and tall chimneys half-hidden by leafless branches, blank windows hiding secrets. There were churches, inns, sprawling manor houses and squat suburban villas, all neatly named and framed, caught in stark black-and-white.

There were other photographs too, still more chilling and mysterious. Kate thought at first that they were just blurry, out of focus. Then she realised. The mist around the fat woman's head was ectoplasm: A milky white substance, pouring from her nose and mouth. The fuzzy effect in the centre of another photo was not due to camera shake, it was a picture of a ghost caught halfway up a flight of stairs.

Davey was nearing the end of his story now. Kate found it difficult to tear her fascinated attention away from the walls and back to her brother. She looked from him to Mrs Craggs to see what effect his words were having on her. The woman was absorbing this tangled tale of ghosts and entities without a single flicker of doubt. Occasionally, she made Davey stop, or repeat something, while she made notes on her yellow pad in loopy flowing writing, but then she waved him to go on again. We've come to the right place, Kate thought. Only here would such a strange tale be believed.

'We heard that you were getting rid of them. The ghosts, I mean. "Cleansing" is the term we heard,' Davey said as he finished. 'We came to see if that was true.'

Sylvia Craggs did not reply immediately. She looked down at her notes, checking through the things that this boy had told her, assessing his story. She saw no reason to disbelieve him. As a medium, she was quick to recognise psychic power in others. Rarely in her life had she come across such ability especially in one so young. To have been to the other side and come back again . . . This was quite exceptional.

'Tell me, Davey,' she said after a while. 'Do you know the term "chime child"?'

'Yes,' Davey avoided her searching gaze. 'Yes, I do.'

Kate looked up. She'd never heard it before. 'What's that?'

'A child born on a Friday, within the chime hours,' Mrs Craggs explained. 'Some say as the clock strikes twelve, others between midnight and cockcrow.'

'What's so special about that?' Kate asked, suddenly nervous. She knew that term applied to her brother. She knew the time of Davey's birth.

'Chime children are gifted. They can see ghosts and fairies . . .' That accounts for a lot, Kate thought. 'They also have immunity from ill-wishing,' Mrs Craggs went on. 'They cannot be "looked over", watched from afar. They love and control animals, they have a way with herbs and healing . . .'

'I thought they were also unlucky—' Davey mumbled.

'Who told you that?' Mrs Craggs' black eyes were sharp upon him.

'Just – someone – someone who knows a lot about folklore.'

Miss Malkin had told him that just before Christmas. Davey shivered as he thought of her. She was the Lady. The Old Grey Man's daughter. She was not a ghost. She was something else altogether. She was a member of the Host, the Unseelie Court. What did Jack Cade call them? Eldritch – fey, faerie. Davey had been careful to leave all mention of her out of his account.

'I have not heard that,' Mrs Craggs said after a moment or two. 'But I do know that chime children are good at keeping secrets.' She gave him a knowing look and her mouth twisted in a half-smile. 'Now, back to the matter in hand,' she looked down at her pad. '"Cleansing" is not a term I would use. I prefer "Banishing".' She stared down at her pad. 'Do not mistake me, I'm no friend to ghosts and spirits. They don't belong in the world of the living. They should move on, travel forward to the place where they belong. But I believe in persuasion. I would not want to force any suffering soul trapped here in spirit. Unfortunately, not everyone in the Society shares this view.' She looked up. 'My colleague, the chap you see pictured there, is keen to use other, more aggressive, methods.'

She nodded towards the newest portrait on the wall, a big colour photograph of a man who appeared to be of indeterminate age, neither old nor young. Formally posed, in a black suit, white shirt and black tie, he looked more like a businessman than a medium. His short dark hair was brushed back from his forehead, his small moustache neatly clipped. Pale eyes stared out from behind gold-rimmed glasses, making him look cold, rather distant. He seemed ordinary, almost nondescript, next to the other more flamboyant portraits.

'Eugene Hutton,' Mrs Craggs waved her hand in his direction. 'Our next President. Very forward-thinking. He has plans for us. He's demonstrating his new method this very evening in front of a *very* carefully selected audience. He wants to take us into the twenty-first century. But I'm too old for this sort of thing,' she indicated the computers and fax machines. 'The Internet and glossy magazines. Look what he's done to our journal!' She brandished the latest copy of *Ghost-hunter*, with its lurid cover. 'It used to be called *Afterword*. I'm leaving. Hence the cardboard boxes.'

'Does that mean you won't help us?' Davey slumped in disappointment.

'I didn't say that, did I?' She regarded him with her dark hooded eyes. 'I am a medium. I *could* open a channel to the other side.'

'Would you do that?'

Davey sat forward, waiting for her answer, relief and excitement rising inside him, but the silence stretched on as the woman stared straight ahead. She seemed to be looking at something over his shoulder, and then Davey felt it, a prickling presence as if someone was standing behind him.

'There is someone who wishes to contact you . . .' Mrs Craggs's normally deep voice became even deeper and her heavy eyelids began to droop. 'A young girl, about Kate's age, dressed in Victorian clothes. She is very agitated. What she has to say is very important . . .'

She stopped speaking abruptly and her breathing took on a heavier, almost snoring quality. Suddenly, she pitched forward until her head was nearly on the desk. Davey turned to Kate in alarm, fearing that the woman might have been taken ill, but his sister motioned him to sit back. Mrs Craggs was going into a trance.

She snapped back, sitting upright in the chair now. Her black eyes were open, but they stared forward, seeing nothing. When she spoke again, her voice was utterly different. The tone was light and silvery, her words quick, rapid with impatience. She was speaking with Elizabeth's voice.

'Davey! Kate! Oh, I'm so glad! I thought that I'd never get through to you. I thought that woman would never stop blathering! Using a human medium is so very tedious!'

'Are you all right?'

'Yes, for now, but there is war in the city, Davey. The Judge is taking his revenge for what happened in the museum. His Sentinels are giving no quarter. He has issued a Declaration, anyone listed is annihilated. But it is not just Sentinels we fear.' Her voice dropped to a whisper. 'There are these others. We call them the Invisibles. They can strike anywhere, at any time, without warning. They are clearing the city of ghosts; soon there will be none left. None!' She broke off, trying to calm herself. 'You have to help us, Davey. You have to make them stop.'

'What happens when the Invisibles come? What happens to you?'

'We disappear.'

'How? Where to?'

'We don't know. No one ever comes back. But it is not what should happen.' Her voice dropped to a whisper. 'It's murder.'

'What about the others? Govan and the Blind Fiddler, Jack and Polly?'

'We were scattered after the clearance of *The Seven Dials*. The Blind Fiddler is less vulnerable than we are. He is not a ghost in the strictest sense. But as to his whereabouts? No one knows. Perhaps he is with the Host. I am with Jack. He is leading the resistance, but things are not going well . . .'

'What about Govan and Polly?'

'There are rumours,' Elizabeth's voice became shaky, indistinct. She paused for a moment. 'Rumours that they have been taken.'

'Taken? Where?'

'The Judge's house. Some are taken and kept there for

reasons that we don't understand. Everything is very confused, Davey. You have no idea. We are harried and hunted, caught between the Judge's Sentinels and the Invisibles. We think they are ghost-hunters from your world, in league with the Judge and the Prior, like Dr Monckton.' Her voice faded to nothing and when it came back it was low and husky, without any of its usual buoyancy. 'If help does not come soon, we are doomed.'

Before Davey could ask anything else, Mrs Craggs' head fell forward on to her chest. She lapsed into deep regular breathing as if she were now asleep.

'What should we do?' Davey whispered to Kate.

'I don't know,' his sister shrugged. 'Wait for her to wake, I suppose.'

Davey leant forward to shake her.

'No,' Kate held his arm. 'It's best to let her come round naturally.'

'How do you know?'

'I read it somewhere. Now keep quiet.'

Davey found waiting and keeping quiet difficult. He could feel the strength of Elizabeth's distress, sense her fear. There had to be a way to help her. He owed his life to her. She had saved him from the Lady.

Mrs Craggs was coming out of her trance now. 'Anything useful?' She asked, fixing the children with her fierce black gaze.

'Don't you remember?' Kate said.

The medium shook her head. 'Never remember a thing. Some mediums do, Eugene for instance, but they have someone on the other side who acts as a spirit guide. I do not. When I'm speaking in spirit, I'm but a conduit. Does a radio remember the words spoken through it? So you'll have to tell me what the girl had to say.'

Sylvia Craggs listened carefully to Kate's account and then sat back in her chair, eyes closed, fingers steepled.

'This Judge's house. Does she mean Judge Andrews?'

'Yes,' Kate replied. 'How do you know?'

'It's the most haunted house in the city.' Mrs Craggs stood up and went to the window and looked over the square. 'Number 1, Fiddler's Court. It even has its own website.' She turned back to face them. 'It's very well-known in ghost-hunting circles. That's why Eugene chose it for this evening's demonstration.'

She handed them each an invitation. Selected guests were invited by Mr Eugene Hutton to see for themselves the effectiveness of his ghost-hunting apparatus and to witness its extraordinary powers.

'How does his system operate?' Davey asked in a quiet voice.

'Not my department, I am afraid,' Mrs Craggs shrugged. 'Haven't got a clue.'

'But it does work?'

'Oh, it works all right. I've seen it with my own eyes.'

'How? How does it work?'

'Some kind of ray we'd have called it in my day, energy force, I suppose. Anyway, this ray, or whatever it is, makes the spirits materialise, and then another one sucks them away again like some kind of psychic Hoover.'

5

'Where is he now? This Mr Eugene Hutton?' Kate asked.

'He was in the building earlier, but I think he might have gone to test his machine.' She reached for a fax. 'We had a request for help from Prima Electronics. Their headquarters are near here. He was thinking of using it for a dry run.'

Davey was not really listening. He was still staring at the address on the invitation. 'This demonstration – we've got to stop him!'

Mrs Craggs shook her head. 'You won't stop him. You don't understand. Eugene is staking his reputation on tonight's performance. There will be all kinds of people here, reporters and journalists, as well as other paranormal investigators. He will not call it off.'

'Why do you want to stop it, Davey?' Kate looked at her own invitation. 'Why is it so important?'

'Don't you see? These "Invisibles" Elizabeth talks about. It's this Eugene Hutton and his ghost-buster machine, it's got to be!'

'Eugene doesn't like the term "ghost-buster",' Mrs Craggs remarked absently.

'What if it is?' Kate frowned. 'If he's using it to get rid

34

of the Judge and the Sentinels, wouldn't that be a good thing?'

'But he's not, is he?' Davey shook his head violently. Kate could be so stupid sometimes. Why couldn't she see? Davey took a deep breath and turned back to his sister. 'Polly and Govan have been collected – to be guinea pigs. Kept with the rest of them, like rats in a lab waiting for Eugene to zap them. We must find a way to warn Elizabeth and the others.' He turned to Mrs Craggs. 'Can you get in touch with her again?'

'I can try,' Mrs Craggs closed her eyes. 'But I'm not a telephone line, you know.' After a moment or two she shook her head. 'No one there, I'm afraid.'

'Oh.' Davey was bitterly disappointed. The only other way was for him to get into the ghost city. But how? The route he had taken before, the mirror in the Room of Ceremonies that acted as a portal, was no longer accessible; the door to it was padlocked. He shut his eyes tight, trying to concentrate. There had to be a way to help them, there had to be; but the more he tried to think of one, the more tangled his mind became and the more hopeless it seemed.

Mrs Craggs watched him closely. She had rarely seen such raw psychic power, but the boy was untrained. He had not learnt to channel his ability. His mind was a prey to strong forces, dragging him this way, that way—

'That's not how you do it,' she said suddenly. 'You

must clear your head. Relax. Empty your thoughts. Dismiss them one by one.'

Her words calmed him, cutting through his confusion. Davey did as she said and gradually felt the tension leaving his body. The surge and beat of each separate thought receded, like surf withdrawing from a beach. At first there was nothing. Then the ghost of an idea came stealing in, and with it, as if born on the wind, the distant sound of a violin.

'Come on, Davey,' Kate was shaking his arm.

'What? What is it?' He felt strange, confused, as if he had been sleeping.

'It's nearly time to meet Tom and Ellie. We have to go.'

Eugene Hutton looked down from the small round window on the top floor of No. 13 Fiddler's Court. Adjusting his gold-rimmed glasses, he watched the two children leave by the front door. He could have gone downstairs to enquire of Mrs Craggs who her visitors were, but he didn't have to. He knew. Anyway, they had been having such an interesting conversation, he would not have dreamt of interrupting. There was nothing paranormal about how he'd heard them, just everyday eavesdropping. An oddity of design in the ancient central heating system meant various sorts of hot air got piped round the building. Most convenient. He did not plan to change the central heating system in his general update.

A tiny smile pursed his small mouth and developed into a little wheezing chuckle as he thought of all the changes he planned to make. He would have no trouble ousting Mrs Craggs. After tonight's little demonstration they would probably make him President for life. He cracked his spidery fingers. His system had taken years to perfect. He had tested it to destruction on every major ghost haunt all over the city. He nudged the large aluminium box by his feet. It was scientifically brilliant and absolutely foolproof.

He'd explained it all to Mrs Craggs, but she was too old and stuck in her ways to understand. She thought it was cruel. He had dismissed her objections as trivial. Ghosts were ghosts, they didn't feel anything. She had completely missed the point.

Tonight's demonstration was all set to make him and his organisation world-famous. He intended to record what happened with special camcorders and cameras, capturing ghosts on film and video for the first time ever. No fakes. No special effects. This would be real. The resulting footage would be worth millions . . .

Behind his gold-rimmed glasses, his icy grey eyes glazed even further as he gazed into a future filled with fame, wealth and success . . . He glanced down at Davey's round dark head as the boy left the square with his sister. The child was smart. Clever. He had guessed correctly at Eugene's intention, but as for stopping this evening's experimentation? Just let him try.

If Davey had been a little less preoccupied, he might have sensed the man spying on him. If he had looked up then, the boy's sharp eyes might have been able to discern a dark form standing by the man's side, hovering by his shoulder, as close as a familiar. Mr Hutton's spirit guide. A medieval monk, known as Prior Robert . . .

Davey did not sense any of these things. He was concentrating his whole mind on trying to read the signs that would point a way into the ghost city . . .

He stopped in the middle of the Market Square and looked around.

'What are you doing, Davey?' Kate pulled his arm. 'We can't stop here. We're late already.'

'I need to find the Blind Fiddler.' Davey replied, refusing to move.

'Can't it wait until we've been to the bus station?'

Davey shook his head. 'There's no time for that. I need to do it now.'

Kate closed her eyes and sighed, mentally counting to ten. Sometimes her brother's behaviour tested the very limits of her patience. She tried to talk to him, reason with him, but he wasn't budging. She looked at him, assessing his stubborn, shut-off expression and felt herself crumble, being forced to give in. She was more practical, more acquainted with the wider picture. Her mind moved along more than one track. She looked at her watch. Tom and Ellie's bus was due in any minute. If there was no one there to meet them, the complications could be awesome.

'Okay, okay.' Kate looked down at her brother. 'You stay here. But wait, Davey. Do not disappear. Do not go wandering off. Are you listening to me?'

'There's just one little thing I want to check out, that's all,' Davey replied. 'It won't take more than a couple of minutes. Then I'll come straight back. I'll be here, I promise.'

Above them the cathedral clock chimed the half-hour.

'You'd better be.' Kate shouted over her shoulder as she went sprinting off.

Davey headed for the great doors of the cathedral as soon as Kate left Market Square. He had not lied to her. Finding the Blind Fiddler, or not finding him, would take only a couple of minutes. What happened after Davey found him, however, could take a while longer . . .

Davey was following his hunch that he would find the Blind Fiddler in or around the cathedral. He wasn't outside, playing his violin, busking in the Market Square, so he had to be inside somewhere. Davey made his way over to the small side chapel that had once contained the shrine of St Wulfric. This was where the Fiddler had been waiting the last time, but now the whole chapel was temporarily screened off.

Davey risked a look behind the plastic sheeting.

'Hello, there.' A boy of about eighteen or nineteen looked up from where he was working. 'Can I help you?'

'Oh, er, I was just wondering why this bit was closed off.'

The boy stood up and removed his protective goggles. White powdery dust smeared across his dark face. He held a chisel and mallet. His callused hands were covered in little scars and nicks, and were so dusty he looked as though he was wearing white gloves.

'We're restoring the shrine of St Wulfric. It's okay, you can come in if you want to.'

'Thanks.' Davey stepped over the threshold. 'What are you doing now, exactly?'

'I'm helping to build the screen to go there, see?' He indicated the recess behind the altar that had housed the original shrine. 'It was smashed at the time of the Reformation. We're making another one. Me and the other trainees.'

Davey looked at the stone tracery the boy was working on. The stone was light, almost blue-white, against the time-darkened grey of the rest of the cathedral. The carving was sharp-edged with clean fine lines. The design of the grille was very simple, plain even, but the delicate carving made it beautiful.

'We're just putting on the finishing touches.' The boy held his arms wide. 'It's got to fit in flush, see?'

'It's fantastic.' Davey walked round the delicately carved screen. 'Brilliant. You're doing a great job.'

'Thanks.' The boy smiled in acceptance of Davey's appreciation. 'But it's not just down to me.'

He turned back to his work and Davey was just about to leave when the boy called out to him.

'Is your name Davey?'

'Yes.' Davey looked back in surprise.

'I just remembered something. There's an old bloke, he's blind, busks violin out in the square. Usually has a young lad with him, but he's been here on his own lately. Anyway, he said to keep a lookout for you.'

'Do you know where he is now?'

'Could be in the Old Garden. Through the door by the Lady Chapel.'

Davey thanked him and left. He found the door and let himself into a walled garden, planted with all kinds of herbs and sweet-smelling plants. Davey could smell sage, rosemary, lavender as he brushed past. The garden was quite a suntrap, it was warm and still and filled with the sound of bees. Davey looked around, thinking at first that there was no one in there, but then he saw the Blind Fiddler sitting on a wrought iron bench tucked away in a corner. He held out his hand as Davey approached.

'Davey! Welcome!' he indicated for the boy to sit next to him. 'I often come here.' His fine nostrils flared to inhale the scents around him. 'It is good to feed the other senses.' He pinched off a shoot from the bush by his side. 'Verbena. Proof against fairies.' He smiled at Davey and held the crushed leaves for him to smell. 'Now,' he spread his thin, long-fingered hands on his knees, 'why did you summon me?'

Davey looked at him in astonishment.

'I didn't know I had.'

'Well, somebody did. Perhaps your powers are greater than you think. What do you want of me?'

Davey took a deep breath before answering. He knew what he wanted to do was crazy. But something was telling him to trust his instinct.

'I need to go into the ghost city. Elizabeth needs me. I

want to help her and the others. I don't know how, but I know I can.'

'Hmm.' The old man thought for a moment. 'Things are bad in the city, very bad. What you propose could put you in dire peril.'

'I know that. But I'm prepared to take the risk. I won't be a nuisance. There's a man involved, a bit like Dr Monckton. I think I know what he's proposing. Having me there, on their side; might even up the chances . . .'

'Perhaps. But your presence might also prove a hindrance. They will have to worry about you as well as themselves. That is why I am here. In your world. They have enough to do without caring for a blind old man.'

'All I want is for you to tell me how to get into the city. I can't use the mirror in the Room of Ceremonies. The door to the underground city is locked. Will you help me?'

The Fiddler did not reply straight away. His blind eyes roved over the sheltered garden, unable to see but taking in the old brick walls, mellow in the evening sunlight, the wide beds of shrubs and flowers laid out round a green lawn, close-clipped and perfect, as smooth as baize cloth.

'You could be putting yourself in considerable danger,' he warned again.

'That is why I want to go alone. Without Kate and the others,' Davey replied. 'Jack's crew have done it for me, risked themselves lots of times, particularly Elizabeth. I owe them a debt.' He searched his mind for a phrase Jack had used. 'A debt of blood.'

'Very well.' The old man leaned forward, his long fingers clasped round the top of his staff. 'Take this path.' He rapped the tip on the ground.

Davey looked down at the brick path beneath his feet.

'Follow it clockwise to the far corner of the garden. There in the wall you will find a door. It is the old Pilgrim's Gate, the way into the cathedral precincts taken by those on their way to the shrine of St Wulfric. Go through the door and you will find yourself where you want to be.'

Davey got up. 'Elizabeth and the others – How will I find them?'

'They will find you. Now go. While we are still here alone.'

Davey did as instructed, keeping his eyes on the uneven brick path, following it round to the opposite side of the garden. When he got to the corner, he looked up. At first he could see nothing. He even wondered if the Fiddler had been lying to him. The wall's face was half-covered in some kind of creeper, but behind that Davey could see that it was blank. Just a mass of small red bricks capped by a roof of coping stones. Then, as he stared on, the wall began to change . . .

Behind the tangle of creeper, a door began to appear, set into a thick stone archway. The arch at the top was round. The bottom disappeared into the ground. It was obviously from a time when the ground here was on a different level. The door itself was made of wood, thick oak slabs studded with metal. At the side was a handle made of twisted iron. Davey stood for a moment, hesitating, then he heard voices behind him. The whole door became transparent and began to fade, shifting like a hologram. It was now or never. Davey took a deep breath. Stepping forward, he grasped the twisted circle with both hands and turned.

7

As Davey stepped through the gate, the world changed around him. He hesitated for a moment, wondering if he hadn't made a big mistake. He looked behind, but the door in the wall was disappearing. It was already too late to go back.

He gazed around, uncertain as to what to do, or where to go. He was in Knowlegate, the ancient roadway that led up from the river, along past the cathedral and into Market Square. A stream of people were surging along in front of him. Men, women, children. Some in family groups, some alone, some carrying bundles and household goods, others walking empty-handed, but they were all heading in the same direction, as if fleeing from something.

As the ghosts streamed past, he noticed that every age and time was represented; it was like watching some bizarre pageant. Normally the ghosts did not mingle. They were divided into crews and they stayed in their own haunting grounds. Something serious must be happening for them to become all mixed up like this. Davey slipped into the throng unnoticed. In his dark T-shirt, black jeans and black trainers, he blended in easily enough. Anyway, the ghosts were too preoccupied with their own troubles to take much notice, that is if they saw him at all. Ghosts did not always see the living, Davey reminded himself; in this world he was the ghost.

He was wondering if any of them could see him, when a woman stopped in her tracks and stared at him, peering up into his face. Then she clutched her shawl closer and backed away.

'You have a look of my son,' she said by way of explanation. 'I search every crowd, every face, just in the hopes . . .' She bit her lip. 'Are you alone?' She looked at Davey again. 'Have you lost your family?' Her worried expression softened into pity. So many had. So many young ones had been separated, left to wander alone since the Cleansing had begun.

Davey shook his head. 'I have no family. I've lost my crew.'

'Come.' She linked arms with Davey. It was her duty to look after him, help him, as any mother would, in the hope that some other mother might be caring for her own son. In the face of the Judge's cruelty, it was all that they could do. 'Come with me,' she repeated. 'It's not safe out in the streets. *They* are coming . . .' She looked fearfully behind her, pale eyes wide, her gaunt face etched with terror. 'We must not be caught out in the open like this.'

'Who? Who's coming?' Davey asked as she dragged him into the ghost tide.

'The Sentinels! They are clearing this part of the city! We must go! We must flee! The curfew bell will soon be sounding. Anyone out after that,' she shuddered, 'can expect no mercy.'

'I'm looking for Jack Cade,' Davey said as they struggled through the crowd. 'Do you know him?'

'The highwayman? I know him by reputation. They say he is gathering ghosts to him in an effort to stem the destruction.'

'Do you know where he is?'

'No, no,' the woman shook her head. 'He keeps on the move constantly. They hunt for him in every part of the city. Clearing it, emptying it, section by section. So far he has evaded their searches. Some say he is to blame for this affliction that has come upon us, but I say all strength to him. He is our only hope.'

At the mention of Jack's name, a man turned towards Davey. He was small and dark, youngish-looking, with long hair straggling out from under a battered cap. His face was deeply scored and marked, his clothes ripped and torn as if he had been in an accident.

'You looking for Cade?' he asked.

Davey nodded.

'I know where he is,' the man smiled, revealing a line of uneven blackened teeth. 'I can take you to him, if you like . . .'

'No, no. It's all right, really,' the woman replied before Davey could say anything. She gripped Davey's arm tighter and hurried on.

'Wait up, Missis.' The small dark man put out a hand to

restrain them. He signalled to others forming around him with a slight motion of the head. 'We've been told to look out for such a one.'

'Then you must be mistaken. This boy is my son.'

The woman pulled on Davey's arm, dragging him again into the thick of the crowd. Davey could hear voices raised behind them, a hue and cry starting. People were surging all around them, pushing and jostling like frightened animals. Up ahead, the way was narrowing. The general flight was about to turn into a stampede.

The woman looked up, sensing the panic spreading around them.

'We must go back. We are entering a trap.'

'How do you know?' Davey looked behind. The road was solid with people.

'The Sentinels. Don't you see them?'

Davey looked up. The way ahead was walled by shadows.

'They set up where the road narrows, forcing the crowd through in ones and twos. Then they can pick off whoever they choose. You have already been selected. That man you were speaking to? He is one of the Judge's own crew. The Recent Dead.'

Davey shuddered, remembering his narrow escape on his first visit to the ghost city. He did not want to be caught again.

'Down here, quickly.' A boy dodged out from the crowd and motioned them to follow him.

The woman hung back, holding Davey to her. The boy turned, beckoning frantically, as the crowd parted. In the distance, Davey picked up the purr of motorbike engines. Motorbikes were the Recent Dead's preferred mode of transport. Davey hesitated no longer. He moved to follow the boy.

'Don't go,' the woman shouted, gripping his arm tighter. 'It could be another trap—'

'I have to take my chances.' Davey gently removed her hand. 'Don't worry. I'll be all right.' He went to go, then turned back. 'Your son. What's his name?'

'William.'

'I'll look out for him. Tell him you're okay.'

'Good luck.'

'You, too.' Davey meant to say more, to thank her, but the woman had gone. The crowd was thinning now, melting away at the edges, dispersing in all directions. It was almost time for the curfew bell.

The boy led Davey into a maze of the narrow alleys that lay behind the main thoroughfare. After the noise and confusion behind, this area was eerily quiet. Davey followed the boy's echoing footsteps. Above his head a single bell began sounding monotonously. That must mean the curfew. Davey had no idea of what lay ahead of him, but nothing could be worse than waiting in line like cattle, trapped between the Recent Dead and the Sentinels with the curfew bell tolling above his head.

8

'Jack sent me to get you,' the boy said when Davey finally caught up with him. 'The Dead ain't the only ones directed to look out for you. Now follow me. We gotta move fast now. Keep close and silent. Ain't safe on the streets once the curfew sounds.'

The boy he was following was about his own age or younger, with a shock of red hair in sharp contrast to his dead-white face. He wore a grey shirt and black trousers shiny with dirt and grease.

'Up here!'

The boy led Davey down between rows of tenements. The buildings were tall, perhaps five or six storeys. They leaned over, almost meeting, allowing only the minimum of light to filter down to the narrow street. Davey had never seen this part of the city. The whole area had been declared structurally dangerous, not to mention insanitary, and had been pulled down many years before he was born.

'This one!' The boy dodged under the sagging eaves, dragging Davey in through a doorway with a splintered frame and rotting lintel.

They ran up and up a tightly turning staircase. The banisters were rickety, missing in places, forcing them to keep into the wall. The stairs themselves were treacherous: the bare boards worn and splintered, some of them loose and broken. The smell of mould and decay was almost overwhelming. The skirting boards were holed by rats and plaster was falling in rotting lumps from the walls.

'Here we are.' The boy whispered, rapping lightly on a door right at the top of the building. 'That's if they haven't had to move again.'

'Who's there?' a voice came back.

'Matty. Matty Groves. I've got a party with me, wants to see Jack urgently.'

'What party?' The door opened a crack.

'The lad called Davey. He's from the Living. He's the one—'

'Why didn't you say straight away?'

The door opened and the man there stepped respectfully out of the way.

'Come with me.' He scuttled off, beckoning Davey to follow him.

Jack's headquarters took up the top floor of the whole block. Rough holes had been knocked through from one tenement into another, providing different sections with different functions: rest area, command centre. The last area was a field hospital. This was where he found Elizabeth.

'Davey!' She jumped up from the patient she had been attending. 'I knew you'd come!'

'What is the matter with them?' Davey looked around

at the wounded lying all about, pale and silent, stretched out on low roughly made-up pallets.

Elizabeth's pretty face changed. All the bright excitement at seeing him drained away.

'Some of them have been caught by Sentinels. Some by the Invisibles. We cannot treat what afflicts them.' She sighed. 'Other than keep them comfortable, there is little we can do.'

'I have news,' Davey said. 'That's why I came. It's about the Invisibles, as you call them. Is there still no sign of Polly?' He looked round for Jack's fiancée, hoping to see her working among the wounded.

'No,' Elizabeth shook her head. Her wide clear brow contracted and her grey eyes clouded with worry. 'Nor Govan. They have almost certainly been taken.'

'What happened?' Davey asked quietly, knowing how much they both meant to Elizabeth. The mute boy, Govan, she regarded as her brother and Polly had been like a mother to her.

'Polly went out after curfew, to help collect the wounded. Govan went with her. Neither of them came back. For a long time we knew nothing. Then word came that they are held as prisoners in the Judge's house. There can be very little doubt. He's trying not to show it, but Jack is beside himself.'

Jack was out on the roof right at the far end of the building. Elizabeth hitched her long skirt above her knees and led the way up the narrow spiral staircase. A door opened out on to a wide flat roof studded with shallow glass domes, put there to shed light into the stairwells below. Jack was leaning over a low parapet, looking through a thin brass telescope out into the darkness descending over the city. Above him the sky contained no stars, no moon, just a deep charcoal greyness deepening to black.

The highwayman turned at their approach and held out his hand in greeting.

'Davey! Welcome!' His dark face was serious, marked with lines of worry and tension, but when he saw Davey his stern expression relaxed into a smile. 'We are in great need of good friends. Tell me, what news do you have?'

'It's about the ones you call the Invisibles . . .'

Jack listened carefully as Davey told him everything he knew about the Society, what he suspected about Eugene Hutton and his special equipment.

'It is as we thought . . .' Jack sighed after Davey had finished. He himself had suspected living ghost-hunters. Nothing else would explain this enemy they could not hear and could not see, prowling the city, striking at any time, at anybody, friend or enemy, as if all ghosts were its foes. 'But just one man, you say?' He shook his head and began walking up and down the narrow space next to the parapet. 'That is hard to believe . . . Where will he strike next, do you know?'

'That's what I came to tell you. He is giving a special demonstration . . .' Davey paused, his heart beating hollow at what he was about to say. 'It's to be held in the Judge's house. He's going to show this machine he has, he's going to use it . . .'

Jack Cade stopped his pacing and stood absolutely still. His dark eyes widened as he stared at Davey and his pale face tightened, flinching slightly as if he had just received a physical blow.

'But not on the Judge, or his evil crew, I'll be bound.'

'No,' Davey shook his head. 'I don't think so. I'm – I'm sorry, Jack . . .'

The highwayman turned from them, and stood for a moment looking out to the far horizon

'You bring grievous news. You must forgive me . . .' He leaned forward, arms spread, leaning over the parapet. 'This man and his machine – what he does is terrible Davey, quite terrible. There is a sound beyond all hearing, it is as if your ears are bleeding. Then, nothing. Anyone, everyone, in the vicinity disappears. Be they one or twenty. There is nothing left. Ghosts are destroyed where they stand. All, all . . .'

He began pacing the roof again, pounding his fist into his hand. Elizabeth and Davey moved together instinctively, backing away from his dark raging fury.

Jack stopped his pacing and looked at them.

'All means Judge and Sentinels. They are ghosts, too . . .' He paused, arms folded, deep in thought. When

55

he looked up, his eyes had lost their look of bleak despair. 'That is one thing we have noticed. Sentinels are never in the vicinity when the Invisibles come to call.' He looked out over the parapet. 'After curfew, there is a lull in their activity, as if they make way . . . but what if it is not that at all? What if they dare not show their presence, because to do so would be dangerous . . .' A hint of a smile lightened his features. 'I begin to have an idea . . .'

Jack called for his lieutenants and was soon deep in huddled discussion.

While he waited, Davey leaned over the parapet, trying to work out where they were in the city as he knew it. He picked up the telescope near his hand and looked out over the surrounding rooftops. They fell away in steps down towards Fiddler's Court. He could make that out plainly, even see the front of the Judge's house. He pulled back as he saw Sentinels like long black shadows stealing into the square, returning from patrolling the city, moving in pairs, dark-robed and hooded, casting black beams left and right.

'The Sentinels are easy to spy on,' Elizabeth said as she stood by his side. 'They never think to look up. That's why we keep to the rooftops.'

Davey moved the telescope round, looking out for other landmarks. Up and to the right lay the cathedral, a dark indistinct bulk of stone in the grim grey gathering night. Down the hill to the left lay the sprawl of little streets that contained *The Seven Dials*. Below that ran Harrow Lane and Keeper's Stairs . . .

Which meant that they were standing approximately . . . The world blurred as he turned quickly to look over the rooftops on the other side. There could be no mistake. Up there was Fore Street, with the law courts and the City Museum. This must be the old Stanley Building, head-quarters of Prima Electronics . . .

'Oh, no,' Davey groaned.

'What's the matter, Davey?' Elizabeth turned, thinking he was physically ill.

'We have to get out of here. Quickly.'

The sickness he felt was at his own stupidity. He had been so concerned about warning Jack about the planned demonstration at the Judge's house that he had completely forgotten what Mrs Craggs had said about Eugene Hutton going out for a trial run . . .

'What?' Elizabeth frowned.

'We've got to go now!' Davey looked round franti-cally. 'Tell Jack! Hutton will be here any minute! Every-one's got to get out!'

It was too late. From below them came a strange low surging boom, like some other sound enormously slowed down. It was almost below the level of hearing, an airborne vibration set at a frequency to break the world and everything in it. Davey felt himself gripped by it, his body, his face, his jaw, even his eyeballs were shaking.

From below came screams and cries and then silence. Across the roof, one by one, the skylights lit up from below with a sickly chemical blue-green glow. The ghost-hunter had arrived.

9

'He said he'd be here . . .' Kate was standing with her cousins, Tom and Elinor, staring at the Market Cross.

'Well, he's not, is he?' Tom looked round, hitching the straps on his shoulders. His rucksack was getting heavy. There was absolutely no sign of Davey. They had looked everywhere, searched the Market Square. The cathedral was closed to the public, so he couldn't be in there. Tom turned back to Kate. He didn't want to seem unsympathetic, but she knew what Davey was like. She must have been crazy to leave her brother on his own in the first place, even for a second.

'He must have gone into the ghost city,' Elinor said. 'Found a way in.'

'How do you know?' Her brother looked down at her.

'I don't, not for sure, I've just got a feeling . . .'

'Don't you start,' Tom snorted. 'One psychic's enough.'

Elinor shook her head. 'It's not to do with being psychic. It just stands to reason. If he isn't here, he must be somewhere else.'

'*Brilliant* deduction,' her brother shook his head in mock wonder. 'Thanks, Sherlock.'

'I think she's right.' Kate said, ignoring his sarcasm. 'As

soon as my back was turned, he must have legged it . . . I knew he was up to something when he wouldn't budge . . .'

'Maybe he's gone back to that Society place you were telling us about,' Tom suggested. 'If he *has* gone into the ghost city, that Mrs Craggs person might be able to tune in to him. She is a medium, after all.'

'She's not exactly a short-wave radio, though,' Kate looked at her cousin. 'What if she can't?'

'Then we'll have to think of something else. Either way, we get to dump these.' He pulled at the straps of his pack. 'My backpack is killing me.'

It was just past seven o'clock, the traditional time for the curfew bell to sound, when Kate, Tom and Elinor presented themselves at the Society's offices in Fiddler's Court.

'What's the matter, child?' Mrs Craggs asked, as soon as she saw Kate's face. 'What's happened? Where's your brother?'

'I – we – don't know,' Kate looked round. Worry was really beginning to gnaw away at her now. 'I thought he might have come back here.'

'Haven't seen him. Sorry. Any idea where else he could be?'

'Well, yes. That's the trouble,' Kate looked at Tom and Elinor. 'We think he might have found a way into the ghost world, the one we were telling you about.'

'Why would he do that?'

'When we left here, he was very concerned about what Elizabeth had told us.'

'Elizabeth is the spirit girl who spoke through me?'

'Yes, that's right. Davey wanted to go and help her and the others, but we had to meet Tom and Ellie. I mean, we couldn't just leave them at the bus station. We – Davey and me – had a bit of an argument. I left him in the Market Square. I made him promise he'd wait there, but when we got back . . .'

'He was gone?'

'Yes.'

'I see,' Mrs Craggs sat at her desk, her large hands clasped together. 'Nowhere else he could possibly be? Tried home?'

Kate shook her head. There was no way he'd go back there, not with all this going on, she thought. It would be hard to phone without giving away that something had happened. Mum'd go crazy if she thought that they had lost Davey.

'If he is in the spirit world,' Mrs Craggs paused to think. 'I might be able to get in touch . . .'

'That's what we were kind of hoping.' Kate glanced at her cousins again.

'Of course, I can't guarantee . . .' Mrs Craggs changed what she was going to say, in response to the distress on Kate's face. 'But I'll certainly try. Now. While everything's quiet. Before our guests arrive and before Eugene

– Mr Hutton – comes back.' She looked at her watch. 'He won't be long. He's only gone to the Stanley Building, just across the back from us. Prima Electronics . . .'

'The computer software company?' Tom asked.

'Yes. Do you know it?'

'Of course,' Tom was surprised that anyone might think he didn't. 'They make games. What's he doing there?'

'Carrying out a trial run before tonight's demonstration. Computer companies have been particularly sensitive during this current wave of activity. We had an urgent request in,' she showed Tom the fax, 'only today. It's the ideal site for Eugene to test the equipment he intends to use tonight.'

'This equipment,' Tom asked. 'What is it exactly? How does it work? Do you know?'

'Haven't a clue. I told Kate and Davey earlier,' Mrs Craggs nodded towards Kate, 'I don't hold with gadgets. My powers lie in other areas.' She turned back to Kate. 'Let's try and contact your brother, shall we?'

Kate, Tom and Elinor sat quiet as Mrs Craggs went through the same routine as before. Once she reached her trance state, Kate leaned forward, on the edge of her seat, waiting for her to speak. But this time Mrs Craggs did not do the strange snoring breathing, or speak in different voices. Her dark hooded eyes blinked a couple of times and she sat back with a shake of her head.

'I can't get through to him or anybody else. I'm sorry,

my dear,' she reached out and patted Kate's hand. 'Trouble and turmoil are creating static. We'll have to try later when things calm down.'

In the world of the dead, no one had time to deal with enquiries from the Living. Ghosts were pouring on to the roof, trying to escape the horror surging up from below. All those who could walk or crawl. The others were destroyed where they lay. Jack Cade was trying to organise an orderly evacuation: trying to quell the panic, dividing the jostling pack into lines across a roof where the skylights sparked and fizzed with bright spurts of light, as if a spot-welder was being used directly beneath them.

Ghosts filed towards the far edge of the roof. From there they were directed by Jack's lieutenants on to the next building and the next, across the city to safety.

Davey helped until there was no one else left.

'Your turn, Davey,' Jack urged him forward gently. 'Off you go.'

Davey looked to the next roof where Elizabeth was waiting for him, beckoning. The space between was not far, perhaps a metre and a half. Nevertheless, Davey hesitated. He was not normally scared of heights, but the chasm between this building and the next plummeted ten metres at least. It made him feel sick. Not just that, the dull booming thud coming up from below seemed to reach deep down inside to the very core of his being, stunning his senses, making him feel weak. Davey could feel his strength draining. He could hardly stand up, let alone leap. He couldn't even see properly. He blinked, staggering slightly. He would have fallen if Jack had not caught him. His arms and legs felt all floppy and he just wanted to lie down.

'Go, Davey,' Jack repeated. 'Go now for God's sake!'

He shook Davey by the shoulder, but the bones seemed to melt under his fingers, it was like gripping an empty sleeve. The highwayman looked down, his dark eyes full of concern, his pale face marked with fear and alarm. This boy was from the Living. He should, therefore, not be harmed by the Invisibles, but Jack knew the signs. The clouding of the eyes, the bluish-green tinge to the skin. It was what happened to ghosts just before they disappeared.

10

All around Eugene Hutton the screens were going crazy. He had warned the company to shut down the system. If they lost files, that was their lookout. Hutton turned off his own instruments one by one and packed them carefully into the different sections of the custom-built aluminium carrying-box. The test run had been satisfactory. More than satisfactory. There was no point in running down the batteries.

He had uncovered quite a nest here. Quite a rookery. The place had been swarming with presences. These were all unseen until he'd brought out his trusty machine, but now he had it all on camera. Eugene Hutton took considerable pride in the system he had perfected. It was of his own devising. A perfect combination of the old and the new. Prior Robert, his spirit guide, directed him to the area of activity; the machines did the rest. It could not be more simple. Eugene Hutton smiled to himself as he picked up the case. He had invented a genuine ghost-busting machine. He disliked the term but it was useful shorthand for what the apparatus did. The results were on film. It was going to make him a fortune. He looked around and saw typical high-tech office premises. There was no outward sign of the devastation and havoc his equipment had wreaked, just a ghostly residue hanging in the air like ozone.

His good humour lasted until he got back to the Society and found those children were back with Mrs Craggs. Not only that, she had invited them to that evening's demonstration. He nodded acceptance of the fiction Mrs Craggs was giving him, that these were her nephew and nieces, but he regarded the three of them with suspicion. The older girl with the long fair hair and pretty blue eyes was the one he had seen from the window. But where was the little dark-haired boy? He had been replaced by two others. A lanky, sandy-haired lad and a girl who was clearly his twin. This was a mystery. Eugene frowned. He didn't like mysteries. At other times, he might have consulted his spirit guide, but Prior Robert was not available to comment. It was too dangerous for him to be near when the machinery was in operation.

Eugene stared down at them, unsure how to handle this. To countermand the invitation might invite suspicion.

'How does it all work, then?' the boy asked. 'Aunt Sylvia has been telling us all about the websites and everything. I'm *very* interested in your invention.' He nodded towards the aluminium box. 'I'd really like to know more about it—'

'I'm afraid that's impossible,' Eugene Hutton replied coldly. 'You'll have to wait for the demonstration, like everybody else.'

'Oh, surely not, Eugene,' Mrs Craggs intervened. 'Can't you give Tom a little sneak preview?'

'No,' he shook his head. 'Like I said. That's impossible.'

'That's a shame. Tom was looking forward to it.' Sylvia Craggs paused, regarding her colleague carefully. 'No one else has seen you use the machine except me. And I'm a bit of a duffer in the technical department. I thought Tom here could explain it to me. People are sure to ask what I think, they always do. Wouldn't want to say the wrong thing.' Her hooded black eyes narrowed on him. 'After all, psychic investigation has been plagued over the years by a great deal of trickery. Wouldn't want you accused of jiggery-pokery – would we now?'

Mrs Craggs let her words hang in the air, allowing Eugene Hutton time to take in her veiled threat. He stared back, his colourless eyes expressionless behind his gold-rimmed glasses as he weighed the possibilities. The old bat might be on the way out, but she still had clout. She could discredit him with the Society before tonight's demonstration had even started. Against that, telling this kid here how it all worked seemed a small price to pay.

'There's not enough room in here,' he said at last.

'You can use your special room upstairs,' Mrs Craggs smiled.

'Come on, then.' Eugene Hutton picked up the

aluminium box and jerked his head at Tom. 'Not that you'll understand.'

Tom grinned at his retreating back. 'Just try me.'

'Thank goodness he's gone,' Mrs Craggs slumped back in her chair with relief. 'Thought for a moment that he was going to dig his heels in.' She leaned forward again, elbows on the desk, fingers tented to her forehead. 'Spirits fairly clamouring, but they don't feel comfortable with Eugene in the room.'

'Is Davey there?' Kate asked.

'Wait a minute, I'll just see,' the woman swayed for a moment, eyes closed. 'He is there. But he can't speak just at the moment.'

'Why not?'

'He's had a shock—'

'What? What kind of shock?'

'That scoundrel you harbour, the Prior's cat's paw, nearly caught him with his infernal machine . . .'

Elinor's mouth dropped open. She had not heard Mrs Craggs speak in trance before. Her eyes widened at the words, the sharp contemptuous tone. The voice coming from the medium's mouth belonged to Jack Cade.

'Is he all right?' Kate asked.

'He will be. He is resting. He has told us all about this Eugene Hutton and his evil machinery. I warn you, Mistress Kate, you must stop this man or we will all be

68

destroyed. Do you know how he brings these terrible things about?'

'Not really,' Kate replied. 'Tom's trying to find out more about how it works right now.'

'Discover all you can. I have a plan . . .'

'What is it?'

'We are to give ourselves up to the Judge.'

'What?'

'I know, I know the risk we are taking, but truth be told, Kate, we have little choice. We cannot resist much longer. Our forces are much depleted, many are injured and wounded. We will be taken soon anyway and now Davey has told us what is intended for Polly and Govan and the others with them—' He broke off and Kate thought he had stopped, but then his voice came back again. 'We cannot take the Judge's house. It is too strongly defended. I had thought to break out from within, like the Greeks and the horse they took to the Trojans, but, since speaking to Davey, I have another idea, but we must work together. Tell me, can you trust this human medium? For much depends upon it.'

'Mrs Craggs? Yes, I think so.'

'Good. Now this is what I propose . . .'

Kate and Elinor listened as Jack outlined his strategy.

'Now I must go,' he said at length, 'there is much to do.'

Kate wanted to ask more, not least about Davey's safety, but Jack's voice stopped as suddenly as it had started. Mrs Craggs was coming out of her trance.

'Well? What happened?' She demanded.

Her voice was as strong and brusque as ever, but Kate could see that the trance had sapped her strength. When she came round this time her face seemed more heavily lined, her eyes a little more sunken, her cheeks bleached of colour.

'Are you all right?' Kate asked.

'I'm fine,' she said, though her hand on the desk was trembling. 'But the experience can be rather draining. Communicating with the spirit world takes it out of one.'

'We spoke to Jack Cade, the highwayman. He has a plan. But he needs our help,' Kate hesitated, 'particularly yours . . .'

'Right. Well, go on. Spit it out.'

'What they propose is . . .'

Sylvia Craggs listened carefully as Kate repeated Jack's plan to her. Far from objecting, she positively relished the prospect. These children had taught her much about a world that she thought she knew already. The ghosts they spoke of – Jack Cade, Polly Martin, Elizabeth Hamilton, the mute boy, Govan – they were part of the city's ghostlore. The Society had files on them all. But she had never thought of them as *real*. She had regarded them as earthbound spirits, and as such they were freaks, anomalies. Interesting subjects for study and research, but with no place in this world. Now she felt differently. They meant no harm, unlike others . . .

She knew about the Judge, too. She knew the story of

'Hanging Andrews' and his Bloody Assizes, how he had sent so many to their deaths, only to meet the same fate on his own gallows. And she knew all about his house. The Society had a file a foot thick on No. 1 Fiddler's Court. She had been there often over the years. Just recently, she had gone with Eugene on his preparatory visit. He had concentrated his attention in the basement. That is where he intended to set up his equipment. She had thought at the time that the room he'd chosen seemed particularly innocent. But there was another room, the one Jack Cade called the Room of Audience. She had been in there, too, on a different visit. It was a conference room now, but even recalling it gave her a shudder. It was as cold as the grave in there. As soon as she walked in, she had sensed something malevolent, hateful, an evil influence exuding malice.

The demonstration would go on, but not, perhaps, exactly as planned. Why should Eugene Hutton have it all his own way? Her black eyes gleamed with satisfaction.

11

Tom came back just as the guests for that evening's demonstration were beginning to gather. Some had come up to the offices to speak to Mrs Craggs, while others waited down in Fiddler's Court. They were an odd bunch. Old professor-types and women of a certain age, like Mrs Craggs herself, obviously lifelong members of the Society, mixed with younger people – long-haired New Age-types – and a sprinkling of what looked like journalists. Kate almost thought to see a TV crew or two. Not this time, Tom informed her. Eugene was saving that for the next demonstration, depending how this one went.

'Did you find out how it all worked?' she asked him.

'You bet,' Tom grinned. 'Me and Eugene,' he held up crossed fingers, 'we're like that.'

'So how *does* it work?' his sister asked.

'You wouldn't understand.'

'Try me.' Elinor looked at him, her eyes glinting impatience.

'First he uses infra-sound.'

'What's that?'

'See – I said you wouldn't understand . . .'

'Give me a chance!' Elinor frowned. 'Explain properly.'

'Yes, Tom,' Kate added. 'We're just as good at science as you are. We just don't show off about it. So get on with it.'

'Okay, okay,' Tom began again, speaking slowly. 'He has this machine that produces very low frequency sound waves. These force the ghosts to reveal themselves. Then he has another machine that sends out electromagnetic pulses. These zap the ghosts right out of existence. The whole process is captured on special film and video using infra-red and digital imaging.'

'How can that work?' Kate interrupted.

'I'm not sure exactly. It's a special recording system designed originally by the military for night operations.'

'I don't mean that.' Kate shook her head. 'I mean how can he zap them? Ghosts are from another dimension.'

'Oh, right. Well, electromagnetism is a very potent force. It can bring down jumbo jets. Ghosts might exist in another dimension, but they exist in the same universe. And it would work on all of them, as far as I can see. I don't see how it could discriminate between friend and foe, nice or nasty.'

'Good,' Kate said. 'We were rather counting on that.'

'What are you talking about?'

'Jack's got a plan.'

Kate left Elinor to explain what it was. Mrs Craggs was

beckoning to her. It was nearly time to leave for the Judge's house.

'I like the idea,' Tom whispered as they crossed Fiddler's Court to the Judge's house. 'Friendly fire.'

'Friendly fire?' Kate had never heard the term used before. 'What's that?'

'It's like in a war when you get whacked by your own side.'

'Oh, right.'

Mrs Craggs turned, motioning them to be quiet. The group were going up the steps and filing into No. 1 Fiddler's Court.

Just as the last person went in, a smartly dressed young woman with silver-blonde hair came up the steps. She looked like a reporter, with a tape recorder over her shoulder. No one challenged her, or thought to see her invitation, as she slipped in through the closing door.

Eugene Hutton took his place several steps up on the wide staircase, ready to address the small crowd gathered in the hall in front of him.

'Any questions?' He looked round at the assembled company after he had finished speaking, rubbing his hands together in satisfaction. His speech had gone down rather well. It had also been pretty comprehensive. The group in the hall looked at each other and then back towards him. 'In that case, without more ado, I suggest we go down to the basement.'

'Just a minute,' Mrs Craggs called up from the back of the crowd. Faces turned towards her. People made way for her as she came forward. She was well known and respected. 'Might I suggest a change of venue?'

'What?' Eugene Hutton was utterly taken aback. He had not expected that. 'But why?'

'You might have the room of your choice rigged in some way.' Mrs Craggs was on the stairs now, addressing the assembled company. She turned to the man at her side, towering over him. 'I would not for a moment wish to imply that you would do such a thing, but it has been known.' She looked down at the people in front and received a few nods of agreement. 'Even if some of us are unconvinced about these mechanical methods, we all agree that this is an important demonstration in the history of the Society.' She paused and got even more nods. Tom smiled. You had to admire how she was working the crowd. 'A *blind* testing, in a room of *our* choosing, would eliminate any suggestion of trickery, avoid the slightest hint of fraud, would it not, Eugene? Surely you agree?'

The people in front of them were turning to each other, muttering agreement. They seemed to decide something between them, almost without speaking. They looked back at Eugene, quiet and expectant. He let his head drop in acknowledgement, knowing that he'd lost.

'Splendid!' Mrs Craggs looked round, confident that the group was with her. 'Now which room?'

'Perhaps we should do a tour?' someone suggested.

'Don't need to,' a small grey-haired man spoke up. 'You want the conference room at the back.' He turned to the others. 'I ought to know. I was a clerk here. All the time I worked here, that room was never right.'

'It does have a reputation,' someone else agreed. 'It used to be the chambers of the old Judge himself.'

'What Judge?' her neighbour asked.

'Judge Andrews. Don't you know about him? Pious as you please by day, busy hanging half the population. Different story by night. Slipping by the side door into Blythe Lane to lead a double life . . .'

'Thank you, Margery,' Sylvia said. Margery Simpson was a fund of local lore and knowledge. She was also a fellow psychic. She had alerted them to the activity at the Tourist Information Office, where she worked as a cleaner. 'Any other suggestions?' Sylvia Craggs looked around. People shook their heads, impatient now for the demonstration to begin. 'Very well. The conference room it is.'

'I'll help you with that, shall I?' Tom stepped forward to give Eugene Hutton a hand with his aluminium box.

'There's really no need . . .'

The man was getting flustered now, sweating. Tom smiled at him.

'It's no problem.'

The conference room was high-ceilinged and long, with a large fireplace of black-veined marble at one end. The walls were covered in wood panelling and rows of tall bookshelves holding volumes of legal histories and case studies. Eugene Hutton directed Tom to put the box down on the long central table. Several people shivered as they entered. This was evidently a 'cold spot'. There was a general feeling among the psychics present that the clerk had made a good choice when he'd suggested this room.

No one sat down. They ranged themselves behind the chairs drawn up to the table, or stood with their backs against the walls.

'I'm not sure that this is going to work . . .' Eugene said as he unpacked his equipment.

'I'm sure it is,' Mrs Craggs remarked with conviction. 'Many of us already feel the presences.' Her fellow psychics nodded confirmation. 'If you want us to believe in what you are doing, Eugene, you had better get on with it.'

Downstairs in the basement, the room that Eugene Hutton had actually earmarked for his experiment was packed to the rafters with ghosts. There were so many in there now that the Sentinels were having trouble keeping order, which was all part of Jack's plan. Polly was here, Govan with her. Elizabeth joined them, going to help the sick and wounded. Davey stayed by Jack, although he wasn't feeling too well himself. The attack had left him weak.

Davey kept an eye on the Sentinels set around the room to guard them. The cadaverous black-robed guards were normally as remote and ruthless as Darth Vader, but now they seemed agitated, upset. Maybe they did not like having to deal with these numbers, or perhaps they had their own problems. Every now and again one or the other of them would look to where the stairs led to the floor above . . .

Of course! Davey thought. They are waiting, just like us. They know. If they get caught, they go, too. He leaned back against the rough stone wall wondering what was happening on the floor above him, and closed his eyes for a moment, concentrating on Mrs C and the others, trying to sense where they might be. Sometimes it worked to try to visualise the scene . . .

Davey opened his eyes. The plan was working. The ghost-hunting party was already in the house, but they were not coming down here. They were being led away to the Judge's Room of Audience. Davey smiled for what felt like the first time that day, and went to tell Jack.

Jack's sombre expression lifted at the news.

'We'll be rid of the Judge, the Prior, the whole crew of them!' He grinned down at Davey. 'We will defeat them yet!'

'Save your breath, highwayman,' a voice sneered above him. '*You* will not be defeating anyone.'

Davey looked up to see Prior Robert. Extremely tall and thin, black robes draped from his skeletal limbs, he towered over them. His eyes gleamed malice from deep inside their fleshless sockets. A lipless grin stretched and creased his death's head face, taking the parchment skin close to cracking. The Prior was chief and most terrifying of all the spectral Sentinels. Davey had never seen him this close before. He flinched back, moving to Jack for protection.

'Do not look to him for help. His days are counted and there will be no returning.' He inclined his hooded head towards Jack. 'The Judge is closing the Book on you and all the rest here.'

He referred to the Book of Possibilities. Within it was recorded: *What Was, What Is, And What Is To Be*. To have the Book closed on you meant to have your name removed. Jack's jaw tightened. That meant you no longer existed.

'The Judge cannot do that,' he replied. 'He does not have the authority.'

'Who is to stop him?' The Prior laughed, a thin rusty creak of a sound. 'Look around, highwayman. The Judge can do as he likes. You have lost. He has won. I cannot tarry in idle chatter. He wishes to see one of you for an audience.'

The presence of the Prior had reduced the ghosts to

hushed silence. The dread word, 'audience,' was greeted with sighs of horror and sharp intakes of breath. Jack stood up, brushing the straw from his breeches.

'Not you.' The Prior pointed a bony finger at Davey. 'He wants this boy here.'

12

'Many hands make light work, Eugene,' Mrs Craggs said, and clapped her hands.

She had felt Davey's presence like a fleeting visitation. With him came the impression that the sooner this was over, the better for all, both living and spirit. She herself did not understand the assembled technology: different kinds of cameras, and the matt black boxes with their various dials, LED counters and digital display screens. There were others present who did, however, including Tom and a young man from one of the paranormal magazines. Since Eugene no longer seemed keen to continue with his experiment, she directed these others to set it up instead.

'Is everything ready?'

The people stationed at various points round the room nodded.

'Wait, wait!' Eugene Hutton stepped forward.

'For what, Eugene?' Mrs Craggs asked coldly. 'Either this works or it doesn't. We are here to find out. If it does, you will be famous. If it doesn't—'

'It's not that!' Eugene's hands twisted in agitation. 'I need to be in touch with my spirit guide . . .'

Eugene had been frantic to contact Prior Robert, to

make sure that he knew about the change of venue. He could sense him in the building somewhere, and coming nearer . . . He only needed to delay for a little longer . . .

'I don't think so, Eugene. Besides, your spirit guide could be damaged,' Mrs Craggs nodded to the machinery. 'You said so yourself.'

'I know but—'

'You told me that this technology supersedes spirit guides,' Mrs Craggs smiled, 'renders such contact obsolete.'

'Yeah,' a young man with a ponytail agreed. 'You wrote an article about that for *GhostWorld*.'

Mrs Craggs smile widened. 'So why do you need yours here now?'

'Well, I, I . . .' Eugene blustered.

'We've wasted enough time,' Mrs Craggs' voice was suddenly brisk and efficient.

'You *can't* proceed—'

'Why not? We don't need your permission.'

'It's my machinery.' Eugene Hutton reached out for the button.

'It's not *yours*, Eugene. The Society funded you.' She looked round the assembly. 'I call upon any members here present . . .'

A forest of hands voted for the experiment to proceed. No one voted against.

'Unanimous. Now, are you ready?' Mrs Craggs looked round, again receiving nods in the affirmative from those stationed at various points in the room. 'Very well.' Hands moved, fingers hovering over various switches and buttons. 'On a count of three. One, two . . .'

The Judge stood in front of his wide table, a white-wigged, black-gowned figure. His fingers rested on the Book of Possibilities closed in front of him; long twisted claw-like fingernails scoring the calfskin binding. His war with the other ghosts, led by Jack and his crew, was finished. The Book was closed upon them. Soon they would no longer exist. Thanks to Prior Robert and the living ghost-hunter. At the last moment, the Judge had sent the Prior to get the boy, Davey. He did not want him caught up in the general destruction. He might have other uses . . .

The Judge paused, interrupting his own line of thought. He looked round his great Room of Audience, his thin nostrils flaring. Something was amiss. He looked towards his assembled Sentinels. They sensed it too and were stirring uneasily. He wished the Prior would return to interpret the changes going on around him. Despite the Judge's great power, he lacked the ability to move between one world and another, but he was sensitive, as all ghosts were, to certain kinds of presence.

He pulled his gown closer, beginning to shiver. The sense of intrusion was getting stronger. A strange deep noise started up. The Judge thought it must be from the cellar, marking the beginning of the Cleansing; but then the candles around him guttered, plunging the room into darkness. The booming sound grew louder. Across the room, his Sentinels sank to their knees, ears covered, mouths contorted in silent screams. A blue-green light sprang up, faint at first but getting stronger, a circle of unearthly fire, eating into the edges of the blackness. The light played across the table, crackling over the Book Of Possibilities, moving over the Judge's robes, outlining his form. The Judge stood transfixed, unable to move, his black eyes reflecting the strange flickering flames. For the first time in his life, he experienced fear.

Seconds before the demonstration began, the young woman journalist slipped out from the back of the crowd. Few people noticed as she glided out through the door. They were too intent on watching the room in front of them, wondering what was going to happen . . .

The Prior pushed Davey up the stone steps from the basement and through the stout wooden door that led in to the main part of the house where the ghost-hunting party was already assembled. Davey deliberately walked slowly, trying to play for time. Once he entered that room, he would be blown away, along with the Judge and everyone else. The Prior gave a guttural growl of impatience and prodded bony fingers into Davey's shoulder, forcing him on.

Davey wondered if he should tell him what he knew.

After all, the Prior would be destroyed, too. It was worth a chance. Even if the Prior did not believe him, even if he thought that Davey was out to deceive him, any delay would be to Davey's advantage.

At the top of the steps, they turned into a stone-flagged ground floor passage made narrow by a number of iron-bound chests and heavy pieces of furniture set against dark wood panelling. Candles flickering inside horn lanterns gave a subdued and gloomy light. Two tall white candles stood either side of a massive oak door, which Davey knew opened into the Room of Audience. He had been here before with Elizabeth and Polly Martin. He glanced to the side. Another passageway led past the stairs to the hall. Beyond that lay the front door. Davey almost made a dash for it, but the Prior's pointed fingers gripped him tightly. The door would be locked and probably guarded. There seemed to be no possibility of escape . . .

'Wait, Prior, wait.' Davey stopped and forced himself to look up into the Prior's ghastly face.

'What is it, boy?' The Prior's voice was gratingly harsh and had a sighing, unearthly quality. It was nearly as horrible as his appearance.

'There's something going on in there.' Davey nodded towards the closed wooden door. He found himself gulping for air, fear made him breathless. 'The – the,' he searched for the word the ghosts used, 'Cleansing – they switched the venue, the place where it's set to happen. The ghost-hunters are in there now. The instruments are all set up, set to go off any minute!' Davey was really beginning to panic. 'Don't you see? If we go in – they'll get us, too.'

'Yes, I see.' The Prior stood for a moment in silent thought. 'That is all to the good. The ghosts held captive there,' he pointed to the basement door, 'will become my slaves. I can be rid of the Judge and rule in his stead. But you—' he looked down at Davey, shaking him like a puppy, 'you—.' The flesh curled back from his lipless mouth. 'The Living have no place here. You have meddled enough in the life of the city. I have no intention of joining them, but you—'

Prior Robert tightened his hold on Davey, half-dragging, half-carrying him. Davey felt like a kitten about to be drowned. Prior Robert's intentions were clear. He held one hand out ready to wrench open the huge oak door. He was going to throw Davey in and then block any exit by pulling across one of the heavy wooden chests set back against the wall.

He was almost within grabbing distance of the door when a young woman came drifting out of the shadows.

'Prior?'

She held up her hand to stop him, and her voice as she addressed him had a cool, quiet, shimmering quality. She wore modern clothing, a short-skirted suit, and had a bag over her shoulder, but Davey knew her, so did the Prior. They both recoiled from eyes that glinted silver and green, like frost on the first spring leaves. It was the Lady. The

Old Grey Man's daughter could change her shape. Appear in any form she liked . . .

'What do you want, Lady?' Prior Robert was almost as astonished to see her as Davey.

She smiled, stepping out of the shadows. 'I care nothing for your petty power struggles with the Judge, or this squabbling between the Dead and the Living. But you cannot have this boy. He is mine. I have a claim on him. Hand him over to me.' She held out her hand with the long silver nails.

'Perhaps I do not choose to.'

'Maybe I can help you change your mind.' Her shark-like smile widened as she looked up at him with tilted narrow eyes. 'I can see to it that you rule here instead of the Judge. Or—'

'Or what?'

'I can make things very difficult. It is up to you to choose.'

The Prior stared. She was the only being Davey knew who would not shrink under his sickly phosphorescent gaze. Their eyes locked in a battle of wills. Davey was a helpless bargaining counter, caught like a pawn between them. She would not let the Prior have what she claimed as hers, but he was not about to give up his prize. Certainly not now that it had increased in value.

'I tire of this . . .'

The Lady was not known for her patience. She leaned forward, lifting the heavy iron latch, letting the big oak door swing open, just a little, so the Prior could see the fate that room held. There was the terrible low booming sound Davey recognised from before. A flicker of sickly blue-green light rippled down the edges of the door. The Cleansing had begun.

The Lady was unaffected. She was not a ghost, after all. She pushed the door open wider.

'You have made your choice, Prior.'

She stood back with a slight smile, watching the Prior warp and morph as infra-sound and electromagnetism combined to rearrange his being. He let out a deep-throated cry, somewhere between agony and despair. His grip slackened, his hand fell away from Davey's shoulder.

Davey was feeling the effects, too. The sound was reaching down inside, numbing his mind. Everything was slowing down, it was like melting from the inside . . .

'Come, Davey,' the Lady held out her long silver-tipped hands to claim him. 'Only I can save you now . . .'

Davey backed away, wanting to escape both her and the door with its crackling blue light. He bumped into something that felt like billowing curtains. He fought frantically as flapping arms wrapped themselves round him like a shroud. The Prior was collapsing, falling in on himself like an empty suit of clothes. Davey struggled to escape from an enveloping blackness that smelt of earth and graveyard mould. Just when he thought that he would suffocate, he managed to heave him off. He pushed the whole scarecrow mess in the direction of the Lady. The

Prior's ragged remnants fell all over her like a toppling marionette.

Davey fled, using what was left of his strength to run up the passage to the front door. There was no one there guarding it. He wrestled with the handle and let himself out, shutting the door behind him with a bang. The more barriers he put between him and that room, the more his strength came back. He paused for just a second before plunging down the steps. He didn't care where he went. He just had to get away. He took to his heels and ran out into the darkening city.

The Lady disentangled herself, stepping over what remained of the Prior with distaste. She made no move to follow Davey. She could have caught him if she had wanted to, but what sport was there in that? He would be hers soon enough. She smiled her silvery frostlit smile. She would not be three times denied, but there were more ways to the wood than one.

13

The party gathered in the conference room watched in astounded silence as the event that they had been brought here to witness unfolded around them. Eugene Hutton's system actually worked! Kate was as stunned as all the rest. The infra-sound revealed another world, in a different dimension, for all to see, not just those with the *sight*. It was like being inside a horror film. As soon as the sound waves were activated, everyone in the room experienced a moment of deep disturbance, supreme discomfort. Cold sweats, hairs creeping up the back of the neck, an awareness of some other presence, the feeling of being watched. Then, just for a second, the apparitions formed. The Judge was there in the room with them, flanked by his Sentinels. All absolutely solid, real, three-dimensional.

Across the room, Tom's fingers worked on reflex, pressing the switch to send out the electromagnetic pulses. No one living felt anything, but they all saw the apparitions begin to warp and contort, convulsing in pain and terror. Then the ghastly vision began to fade, slowly at first, then more quickly, until there was nothing. Tom stared at the place where the Judge had been standing. He would never forget those cold black eyes, staring back at him, hollow with horror, at the final moment of understanding when the Judge met his nemesis.

Then it was all over. The witnesses began to file out, discussing what they had seen in the hushed tones of those who knew themselves to have taken part in something special. The event would become a legend among those interested in paranormal phenomena; but it would not be without controversy. Arguments were breaking out already. Nobody could agree that they had all seen exactly the same thing. Even the video footage and the film exposed would not convince some people. Debate was set to rage. Some swore that they saw a room in another time, a different dimension. The Judge, white wig and all, standing before a table, his hand on a great book, the robed and cowled figures of monks standing around him. Others said that they saw nothing like that, merely dark shapes and formless figures that could have been anything. Despite this, everyone agreed that something had occurred. Hutton's apparatus certainly worked. His reputation was assured. The series of stills and the footage he had on film was already worth a fortune.

He was surrounded now by a small admiring group mostly from the younger crowd. Mrs Craggs nodded at one or two and ushered the children past them.

'What about Davey?' Kate whispered when they got to the hallway.

Mrs Craggs said nothing, but led them out into the quiet little square. At the centre was a fenced-off part for residents only. A tiny patch of grass, a scattering of benches and a small play area showed through a group of trees. Rowans and silver birches, their slim trunks gleamed grey and white in the shadowy darkness. Mrs Craggs groped in her bag for a bunch of keys and, finding the right one, felt for the lock on the wrought-iron gate, turning the key to let them in. She went to the nearest seat and sat down, immediately closing her eyes. She looked old and tired, as if the whole experience was proving a little too much. The children stood in front of her, ranged round in a semi-circle. They exchanged glances. Perhaps she had gone to sleep. Perhaps . . .

Her mouth opened and closed like a fish, Kate stepped forward, convinced this time that there was something seriously wrong. Just at that moment, the woman began to speak, but not with her own voice. Elizabeth was speaking through her. The ghost girl's voice was in stark contrast to Mrs Cragg's old worn face. It was vibrant, full of joy and excitement.

'They are gone! All gone! The Judge and all his crew. What a trouncing you gave them! It is like a miracle . . .' Her tone changed to awe. 'We cannot quite believe it. We are free! The city is ours! I must go. There is much to do. All I can say now is thank you.'

'Elizabeth!' Kate spoke. 'Wait!'

'What is it?'

'Where is Davey?'

'Is he not with you?' The ghost girl sounded puzzled. 'When he did not come back and the great change came about, we assumed—' There was a catch in her voice. 'You don't mean . . . surely he wasn't caught up in the Cleansing along with the Judge and his cohorts?' Her tone turned to anguish as she realised what could have happened.

'No,' Kate said, quick to reassure her. 'We don't think that. He wasn't in the room when it happened. It's just . . . well, he's not here . . .'

'Oh.' All the jubilation left Elizabeth's voice. 'I see. Well, I'm afraid that he's not here, either.'

Davey did not even look to see the direction in which he was heading. He just ran on and on, letting his feet take him where they would. Eventually he had to stop to get his breath. He leaned against a wall, still not really taking any notice of his surroundings, only gradually becoming aware of the bulk of the cathedral towering above him. He looked up now, recognising the narrow winding street as Knowlegate, the lane that ran down by the side of the cathedral. He traced along the wall, fingers running over its rough brick surface, until he found a door. His heart skipped a beat as he recognised the low weathered stone arch and the grey pillar supports, all worn and wasted, eroding away to sand. The latch in the door felt as thin as paper, half-eaten through by rust. With trembling fingers he moved it up and pushed on silvered wood, polished smooth by the pressure of many palms. The door swung open, letting him into the garden.

He stepped on to the brick path and pale moths fluttered up all around, rising from petals glimmering white in the gathering darkness. The door closed behind him and Davey stood quiet, breathing in the heady complex scent of many herbs and flowers.

He looked round warily and then relaxed. He was back in his own time. Crisp packets and plastic sandwich boxes stuck out of the top of a litter bin. A small metal notice warned: 'Keep Off the Grass'. Something told him that he would be safe here. He walked to a nearby bench and sat down. His legs felt wobbly all of a sudden. So much had happened, first with the ghosts, then the Lady . . . He was so tired. He didn't want to think about it now.

It wouldn't hurt to rest, just for five minutes. He lodged his elbow into the corner of the curved iron arm and, using his hand as a pillow, he closed his eyes, never doubting that he would be safe from enemies, whether they were ghosts or fairies. Nothing could harm him here.

He woke suddenly, with no idea where he was, only knowing that someone was shaking him. Davey looked up and his alarm turned to terror. A tall figure dressed all in black was towering over him. He thought for a second that it was Prior Robert, escaped and come after him, pursuing him even into his own time. He tried to squirm out from under the gripping hand, backing away, flattening himself against the bench.

'It's all right. It's all right . . .'

The voice was deep and calming. The hand on his shoulder was large but gentle. Davey took a deep breath and felt his heartbeat settle. He was not looking at a spectre. This was a man. He was tall and was wearing long black clerical robes, but the hand on Davey's shoulder was warm and the eyes gazing down were blue and kind.

'I didn't mean to alarm you,' the man was saying, 'I just wondered what you were doing here. It's late and the cathedral is closed.' He pushed a hand through his thick shock of white hair and looked at Davey for a moment. When he spoke again, his voice was even quieter, his tone filled with compassion. 'Have you nowhere to go?'

'Oh, no.' Davey sat up, catching his drift. The man must think he was homeless. 'I mean, yes. My name is Davey – Davey Williams. I live in Wesson. Wesson Heath.' He found himself parroting his name and address as if he was five. 'I – er – just,' he looked around at the quiet garden swamped in shadow, 'I must have just fallen asleep.'

'Oh, I see. Good thing I happened along, then. You could have been here all night.' He held out his hand to help Davey up. 'My name's Michael, Michael Campion. Pleased to meet you Davey. I'm Provost here.'

They walked round the garden to the gate opposite. Normally this was locked but the Provost had the key for it.

'There has been a garden here for many centuries,' he said. 'I like to think it goes back to St Wulfric. The monks planted herbs for their medicines and for the kitchen, but also for the beauty and scent they gave and the insects they attract. I often slip in here on a still night like this. I find it a good place to think. Now,' he looked down at Davey, 'we'd better see about telling your mum where you are and getting you home.'

Alison Williams, Davey's mother, was not too impressed about making two trips into the city, first to get Davey, then to collect Kate and his cousins. She accepted that it was a genuine mix-up, but they were still very late and she had been worried. As the eldest, and therefore the most responsible, Kate caught the worst of it. But it was her birthday the next day, and there was no point in going on too much and spoiling the occasion for everyone. Not now that they were all back safe and sound.

14

Every year, on May Bank Holiday, the fair came to town. It had done so, around about this time, for centuries. It was a genuine funfair, with rides and sideshows, set up in the very heart of the city, the streets cordoned off all around. Because it was near her birthday, when she was small, Kate had thought that it was there in honour of her. She now knew better, but she had adopted it anyway as an unofficial extension of her own celebrations. The twins usually stayed over to join in with Kate and Davey and their friends. They would all go into the city together in one great big gang.

This had once been a horse fair, a trading fair, and still attracted people from everywhere. Itinerants of every kind: gypsies, tinkers, hippies, New Age travellers, traders, conmen, tricksters, musicians. The Blind Fiddler had come as a young man with his violin under his arm, and bright blue eyes like chips of turquoise, and had never gone away. The Great Fair, as it was known in those days, attracted others. May Day, the old Celtic festival of Beltane, is one of the hinges of the year. One of the special times when the fabric between the different worlds grows thin. The fair began in the hours of twilight and went on until midnight. Twilight is one of the hinges of the day.

The streets were crowded and not just with the Living. This was one of the nights when ghosts could join the jostling crowd and this year they were there in force. They had something to celebrate, after all. They were finally free from the Judge's tyranny. In honour of this they were holding their own great gathering and it mattered little to them that the gathering place was right in the middle of the fairground.

The more acceptable-looking ghosts went on rides and had a go on the coconut shies, just like their human counterparts. Those too ghastly to pass had their fun somewhere else. They took their places in the Ghost Train and Haunted House. Genuine ghouls lurked in among the plastic skeletons and painted spooks, shrieking and swooping as the train rattled past. Customers came out of the swinging doors, wide-eyed with wonder or shaking with terror. Side-show holders scratched their heads as they received complaints and compliments about things that just shouldn't be there.

The ghosts fitted in so well, that even Kate failed to notice them, until a hand tapped her on the shoulder and a voice in her ear said, 'Good evening, Mistress Kate.'

Kate turned to find Jack Cade standing by her side. The highwayman did not look out of place. In white shirt and black breeches, dark hair tied back with a ribbon, and a scarf looped loosely round his neck, he looked as though he could be selling jewellery on one of the hippie stalls.

His dark eyes sparkled as he asked her, 'How do you enjoy the fair?'

'Great,' she smiled up at him. 'I love it. We come every year.'

'So do we.' He returned her smile.

'I've never seen you.'

His grin widened. 'That is because you've not been looking.'

'Where are the others?'

Kate gazed round her and suddenly she saw Govan and Elizabeth smiling at her and Polly browsing on a nearby stall.

'There are many of us here,' Jack smiled. 'It is our last great gathering. We are leaving the city.'

'When?' Kate was shocked to hear that.

'Soon. Midsummer's Eve. Now the Judge's power is broken, we are free to go. You must come to the city then, so we can say farewell.'

'Oh . . .'

Jack looked down at her. 'Don't sound so sad and disappointed. Our time has come. You should be glad—'

'I am, of course, it's just—' To Kate's surprise, she felt tears welling up inside her. 'I'll miss you. All of you. You've been our friends—'

'Hold, Mistress Kate,' Jack Cade laughed and shook out a snowy-white handkerchief. 'We have not gone yet.' He looked around as Kate blew her nose. 'Where is Davey? Is he not with you?'

Kate turned, surprised. He'd been right by her, not a minute ago.

'He must have gone off by himself somewhere,' she said.

'Oh,' Jack frowned. 'I was thinking to warn him . . .'

'About what?'

'There are folk of all sorts here, not just ghost and Living—'

'I don't follow . . .'

Kate's shake of the head forced the highwayman to be more explicit, although he was loathe to speak of them, especially here and at a time such as this.

'I mean the Host.' He dropped his voice and drew nearer, as though not wishing to be overheard. 'I speak of the Lady—'

'She's here?' Kate looked round in alarm. 'Right now?'

Jack nodded. 'And not alone. She will have others with her. The fair folk love a fair.'

'What does she want with Davey? I thought that she'd forgotten—'

Jack gave a hollow laugh. 'Her kind never forgets. They bear grudges for centuries.'

'What will she do to him?'

'I don't know,' Jack shrugged. 'But she does not wish him well, you can depend on that. I will alert the other ghosts and we will look out for him as best we can. Meanwhile my best advice is to find him and get him away before they can do him harm.'

'I certainly will,' Kate frowned. 'Thanks, Jack.'

'Think nothing of it. All the ghosts have a special care for Davey. He is quite a hero, you know.'

'Was that Jack?' Tom asked when Kate got back to her cousins standing by the dodgems.

'Yes. Have you seen Davey?'

Tom shook his head. 'But we just met Elizabeth, didn't we, El?'

'She said the Lady was about and to look out for Davey.' Elinor shivered. She had seen the Lady only once, at Hallowe'en, but once was enough. Just thinking about her was enough to bring on a panic attack. 'We have to find him, and fast.'

She looked round, eyes searching the crowds. Next to Davey she was the most sensitive. The other two regarded her with alarm.

'What do you mean, El?' Kate asked.

'I'm not sure.' She hugged herself and shivered again, even though the night was warm. 'I just have a feeling, that's all.'

Normally Elinor's 'feelings' sent her brother off into a fit of scoffing. Not this time.

'What's it telling you, Ellie?' he asked her gently.

'That if we don't hurry, we'll be too late.'

Elinor looked up at her brother, the expression in her eyes turning to fear.

'Okay,' Tom turned to Kate. 'Where did you last see him?'

Kate indicated over by the waltzers.

'We'll start there and comb right through the fair. One end to the other. Sticking together. All right?'

They set off, arms linked, Tom looking straight ahead, Kate to the left, Elinor to the right. They scoured the stalls and the arcades, the sideshows and different attractions scattered through the streets all around. But their searching was concentrated on the ground; it did not occur to any of them to look up for quite some time . . .

Davey loved fairs and this was his favourite. Although the rides were fewer and small in comparison, for him it beat theme parks or seaside fairgrounds. He loved the hot smell of candy floss and diesel and he loved the way the streets were taken over. All normal life was swept aside in the rush and swirl of the rides, the bright garlands of garish lights and the brash echoing boom of music hugely amplified.

He'd lost the others ages ago. He liked to savour the fair alone, to go round on his own, sampling this and that. The day had been warm and bright, and was just fading into night. He stood breathing in the atmosphere, the rich mix of conflicting smells. To the diesel oil and candy floss, he added onions, burgers and hot dogs. Above him, riders shrieked and whooped, swooping through the gathering darkness, calling like high strange birds as their carriages twisted and turned through snaking necklaces of light. It was like stepping into magic.

He longed to go up on the rollercoaster, but the fare was dear, and he didn't have any money left. He felt in his pockets. His sampling had taken quite a toll on his finances. He was all spent up. He was just about to troop off miserably when he noticed something down on the ground. A tightly folded wad of paper glinting orange and bronze in the gutter. He bent down, thinking it was a discarded ticket from one of the stalls, but his fingers unfolded a ten pound note. Davey looked around furtively, thinking he should hand it in to somebody, but knowing he had no intention of doing so. He folded it back into the palm of his left hand, ready to give it to the man who ran the ride.

Someone opened the door. Someone else flipped up the bar and Davey got down from the car. His legs were shaking. He came out past the pay booth to find Tom waiting for him. Tom had finally sussed that he could be on the ride and had been there to meet every car. Tom frowned as Davey came towards him down the ramp. He was holding on to the rail like a little old man.

'Wow!' Tom commented. 'That must have been some ride!'

His cousin's face was pale, the freckles stood out like

dots sprayed across it. His eyes, wide and black, seemed all pupil. He looked like he was about to throw up.

'Yeah,' Davey replied in a whisper. 'Yeah, it was.'

'How long have you been on it?'

Davey did not reply, just shrugged.

'You the only one to get off?' Tom looked past his cousin. No one else was with him.

'Yeah. The others must've paid to go again.'

Tom looked up. The car crawling up the steep incline to the start of the ride was empty.

'Are you sure, Davey, mate?' He nodded his head towards the rollercoaster track. 'It looks like there's no one in it to me.'

'Sure?' Davey turned slowly, his eyes still dilated and unfocused. 'Of course I'm sure . . .'

Davey would never forget that ride, or those who had ridden with him. They had enjoyed it as much as he had. Their slanting eyes had glittered, igniting with excitement as the car plunged and twisted round the track. Their high wild cries seemed to make it go faster, as if they could make it take off. They rode standing, arms out as if they were flying, their hair streaming behind them like wind-blown fire.

'Are you all right?' Tom asked, his sandy brows drawn together in a puckered frown.

'Yeah. 'Course,' Davey looked back at him. 'Why shouldn't I be?'

'No reason,' Tom shrugged. 'Let's find Kate and El.'

104

'Okay.'

Davey followed Tom obediently enough, but Tom thought his cousin was acting strangely, even for Davey.

Kate thought so, too. She phoned her dad to come and get them. They had all had enough of the fair by then. Their father arranged to meet them over the bridge in the New Town. Davey didn't object. He followed his sister and cousins meekly, but every now and then he would turn to sneak a look at the snaking, twisting rollercoaster lights and to listen out for the shrieks and cries from the ride. He had never been so excited in his whole life as he had been up there in the sky. He had never seen people like the ones who had ridden with him, with their long flowing hair and slender limbs and shiny clothes of silver, gold and green.

Maybe they were in a rock band or something, Davey thought to himself. That must be it. There was to be a concert later on, with laser lights and everything. Kate had nagged and nagged at Mum and Dad to be allowed to go, but they had said 'no', she was still too young. Davey had not been bothered, until now. He just wanted to see those people again. Be with them. His heart ached with a longing he had never known before. Everything around him meant nothing. They had been so glamorous. That was the word for them, he decided. Glamorous.

Glamour is an old, old word meaning to bewitch or enchant, but Davey did not know that. Neither did he realise that a glamour had been cast over him. He had stepped from the earth into the air and met the creatures who dwelt there; now he was caught in their deep enchantment, fluttering like a moth inside a lantern.

Midsummer

1

'Kate, Kate!'

Kate Williams turned, surprised to hear her name being called. She pushed her fair hair back from her damp forehead and squinted into the bright sunlight, peering through the end of day crowd jostling out of the school gates. She was even more surprised to see Lisa Wilson, one of her brother's friends, jump off the fence and come running towards her. Although their schools were on the same site, Kate was fourteen and went to a different part to Davey. The Senior School had a different finishing time, so Lisa must have been there for at least twenty minutes.

'Can I have a word with you?'

'Yes, sure.' Kate stood, bag balanced on hip, waiting for the younger girl. It was a hot day in the middle of June and her summer uniform shirt was sticking to her back. The sun had been beating against the glass windows of her classroom all afternoon, but it wasn't much cooler outside.

'What's up?' she asked as Lisa joined her.

'It's about Davey,' the other girl replied, but would say no more until they were through the throng waiting for buses and lifts.

'What about him?' Kate asked as they took the path that

led across to Derry Hollow and up to the Puckeridge Estate where they both lived.

Lisa hung back, making sure there was a good wide space between them and the little knot of girls walking along in front of them. She looked round before she spoke, to see that there was no one coming up behind them. It was clear that whatever she wanted to speak about was private.

'It's about Davey . . .'

'You said that already. Look, Lisa . . .'

Kate looked down at the other girl, thinking that she knew where this might be heading. Lisa and Davey were good friends, close friends. They saw each other all the time. They sat next to each other in class. Relationships started young these days. When she was in Year Seven, loads in her class had been going out with each other. Kate could sympathise, but she did not want to act as some kind of Agony Aunt sorting out her younger brother's love life.

'I don't know how it is with you two,' she went on, 'and frankly I'm not sure I want to, but, well, maybe he's a little too young. Boys mature later than girls . . .'

'What are you talking about?' Lisa looked up at Kate, her grey eyes puzzled, black brows drawn together in a frown. 'Oh, no,' she added, colouring as she realised what Kate was getting at. 'Oh, no,' she repeated, shaking her head for emphasis. 'It's not that. It's *nothing* like that!'

'Oh, right.' It was Kate's turn to blush at her own misunderstanding. 'What is it then?'

110

'He's been acting strangely, that's all.'

'In what way?'

'Well,' Lisa frowned again, trying to think how to describe it. 'He's kind of not there half the time, like he's on a different planet . . .'

'So?' Kate grinned. 'What's new?'

Lisa shook her short dark curls. 'This isn't the same. He just doesn't seem interested in anything. Like – we started this project together at the beginning of term – about The Crusades – and he was all fired up about it to start with – got loads of books did lots of work, but just lately he's done nothing, left it all up to me.'

'Well, that's the problem with projects . . .' Kate said vaguely. She didn't want to get involved in petty work squabbles, either. She wasn't her brother's teacher.

'Don't get me wrong,' Lisa corrected her. 'I don't *mind* doing it, it's just, it's just not like him. We've done tons of projects together and he never shirks his part of the work. It's like something's turned off inside him. He's just not interested in anything. He goes off on his own, like at lunch and breaktime, and he never calls for me, you know, to walk to school, and he's out as soon as the bell goes. It's not just me,' she added quickly, in case Kate began to get the wrong idea again, 'he's avoiding everybody. I mean, he's never hung around with a gang, but he's not a loner. He's always been sociable, up for a game of football and that, but now he never joins in anything. Haven't you noticed?'

'Well . . .' Kate stopped for a moment to consider whether to tell Lisa what was essentially Davey's business, 'yes,' she said eventually. 'He's been behaving the same way at home. He's been losing weight, too. Don't say I told you, but Mum's even taken him to the doctor to find out what's wrong with him.'

'What did the doctor say?'

'Nothing,' Kate shrugged. 'Couldn't find anything. Gran puts it down to "outgrowing his strength" and says he needs a tonic. Mum's been muttering about "growth spurts" and hormones and dosing him with vitamins.'

'He has been getting thinner,' Lisa agreed. 'Maybe that's why he looks different.'

'How do you mean, different?'

They were coming out of the entry where the path came into Derry Hollow. From here, their homes lay in different directions. Lisa lived in Garden Court, a block of maisonettes off to the left up Puckeridge Rise. Kate's house was on Derry Way, which led up to the right. They stopped in front of the wide drive leading down to Derry House. The tall Victorian house at the bottom of the estate had been empty for some time. It was still creepy, despite the fact that someone had finally bought it and builders' vans stood around on the buckled tarmac. The windows were boarded and plastered with signs; blue plastic shutes snaked down from the roof to a series of skips. But, even on a day like this, the house seemed all in shadow, the air around it chilly. Kate rubbed her arms. It was definitely what Mrs Craggs would call a 'cold spot'. Kate shuddered. She did not like to linger here, despite the hot brightness of the day. She still had nightmares about what had happened in there at Hallowe'en. First to Davey, and then their confrontation with the Lady. She had a feeling that whoever bought it, and whatever they did to it, the building would always belong to her, it would never lose its brooding atmosphere of ancient malice.

'Well,' Lisa was saying, 'his face looks thinner, especially since he had that haircut—'

'Pardon?' Kate had been so lost in thought that she had forgotten what they were talking about, or even that Lisa was with her.

'Davey. You asked how he looked different.'

'Oh, yeah, right. I'll check on him. Don't worry . . .' Kate suddenly seemed in a hurry to go.

'That's not the only thing.' Lisa caught her arm. 'It's his eyes—'

'His eyes?' Kate stopped and looked down at the other girl. 'What about them?'

'I could be imagining it . . .' Lisa started, knowing how strange this was going to sound, 'but they seem to be going a different colour.'

'A different colour? What on earth do you mean?'

'I don't know, exactly.' the younger girl shrugged. 'It's, it's hard to explain . . .' She thought about Davey's

113

distinctive dark brown eyes. 'They seem to be getting lighter.'

Kate frowned, bringing her brother's face to mind. There did seem something odd about it. Weight loss and a new haircut could certainly account for his changing appearance – but his *eyes*?

'You have to be mistaken, Lisa.' She shook her head, not really wanting to acknowledge what the girl had said. 'People's eyes do not change colour.'

Kate's voice sounded loud, echoing off the houses on the quiet estate. In the silence of the hot afternoon it seemed to be followed by another sound. A high silvery chuckle. Kate looked round. The hair was like fur on her arms now. The laugh was coming from the Hollow. It could be a radio, or one of the workmen, but it sounded light, like a woman's voice, and it didn't sound human. Kate had heard the high ringing tone before, in the basement of Derry House.

2

When Kate got in, Davey was sitting at the kitchen table flicking over the pages of a magazine. He barely looked up as his sister entered the room, but that wasn't unusual. They quite often ignored each other as they went about the routines of family life. Kate got herself a drink and something to eat and sat down opposite him.

'Mum in yet?'

'No.'

'How about Emma?'

'Upstairs.'

'What are you going to do tonight?'

'What's it to you?' Davey held his football magazine up higher.

'Just wondered if there was anything good on the telly.'

'How should I know?' Davey concentrated his attention on an item at the bottom of the page. 'Go and get the TV guide.'

Kate went and fetched it out of the living-room.

'Just repeats,' she said as she studied the page. 'Maybe we could get a video. There are a couple of new ones out. We could go down the video shop and have a look, get some coke and popcorn—'

'You do what you like,' Davey cut her short. He folded his magazine and stood up. 'I've got things to do.'

'Oh,' Kate's voice remained level. She didn't want to show how his abrupt rejection had stung. 'Like what?'

'Homework. I've got a project to finish.'

He left the room without a backward glance. There was no chance to check on the colour of his eyes. He hadn't even looked at her.

Kate went upstairs. Davey's door was firmly closed. She thought about knocking, but went on past. He might get suspicious if she paid too much attention and she didn't want to spook him, or get Lisa into trouble. She went into her own room and lay on the bed, trying to think of a different approach. After a moment or two, there was a small knock on the door.

'Come in!'

'It's me,' Emma, Kate's younger sister, came into the room. 'I want someone to listen to my reading. I asked Davey, but he told me not to bother him; said that he was busy . . .'

Emma hung back by the door, not wanting to invite another refusal.

'Come on in,' Kate smiled, 'I'll have a listen.'

Kate patted the bed next to her. Emma extracted her reading book from the battered ziplock bag that she had been hiding behind her back and came to sit by her sister. She flattened the book out on her knees, holding it open

116

at the right place. Her recently cut chin-length bob fell forward, shading her face. She read using her special, careful 'reading book' voice, pointing each word out with a stubby finger and beating out the rhythm with her heels. Emma was eight, but tall for her age. Her long legs were brown from wearing shorts all the time, and scabbed and scratched from playground falls.

Kate looked up and caught a glimpse of them both, side by side, in the mirror. They were like each other in looks: the same slim build, silky fair hair and cornflower-blue eyes. It was the kind of similarity constantly remarked upon by relatives, teachers, friends of the family. Davey had always been the odd one out; as compact and dark as they were willowy and fair. He didn't really look much like Mum, or Dad either, for that matter. 'Where did he spring from?' people would joke. As though he didn't fit with the rest of them. As though he'd been swopped at birth – like a changeling . . .

'You're not listening,' Emma complained.

'Yes, I am.'

'What's it about then?'

Kate took a quick squint at the cover. 'It's about a little boy who's lost his dog.'

It wasn't entirely a wild guess. A lot of Emma's books seemed to involve children who mislaid their pets.

'Hmm,' Emma was still suspicious. 'Where does he find it?'

'I don't know,' Kate shrugged her shoulders. 'We haven't got to that bit yet.'

'All right.' Emma seemed satisfied with that answer. She grinned, her new front teeth looked too big in her elfin face. 'I'll read some more, then. We are supposed to do at least as far as the next bit or Mrs Thompson gets cross.'

'Yeah, sure. Read to the end if you like.'

'Oh, no,' Emma shook her head, serious again. 'You mustn't do that. She gets cross if you do that, too.'

'Whatever,' Kate leaned back. 'Do as much as you want, and then I want to ask you something.'

'What did you want to ask me?'

'What?' Kate had been lying back on the bed, almost asleep, lulled by her sister's reading.

'I've finished my reading,' Emma explained patiently. 'You said you wanted to ask me something.'

'Oh, right,' Kate struggled up. 'It was about Davey.'

'What about him?'

'Have you noticed anything . . .' Kate thought for a moment, wondering how to put this, '. . . well . . . odd about him lately.'

'No,' Emma shook her head. 'He hasn't been horrible, if that's what you mean.'

Emma was nearer to Davey in age. The two of them tended to squabble and fight much more with each other than they did with Kate.

'You mean he's being nice?'

'Not exactly. He just ignores me,' Emma stopped to

118

think. 'No, it's more than that. He lets me watch what I want on TV, he even lets me play with his things. It's like he can't be bothered. There's something else . . .' Emma looked at her sister, wondering whether to say.

'What?' Kate hugged her knees.

'Well, it's at night . . . I hear him sometimes.'

'Hear what? His stereo?'

Emma's room and Davey's were separated only by a thin partition. He'd been told off before for disturbing her.

'No,' Emma shook her head again. 'I hardly ever hear that. I don't think he plays it any more. It's, well, I hear noises . . .'

'What kind of noises?'

'First off, I thought it was ghosts, like in the dream I had at Hallowe'en. Oh, I know I was silly and they weren't real,' she added quickly, misinterpreting the concern on Kate's face. 'And I don't believe in them any more, not really, but when I heard the noises, I thought of them.'

'But it wasn't them?' Kate asked weakly.

The ghosts at Hallowe'en had been real enough, but Kate thought that Emma had forgotten the hideous clown and his ghastly crew. She thought that Emma accepted that they were just figures from a nightmare. Now she was forced to wonder exactly how much her sister did remember.

'How could it be? They don't exist!' Emma said, to

Kate's relief. 'Sometimes you are silly, Katie!' she added with a grin. Her new teeth gave her a slight lisp. 'No,' her bobbed hair swung out and back again, 'it was Davey.'

'What was he doing?'

'Getting up and padding about, in his room and around the house.'

'That's not so unusual,' Kate said. 'It has been very hot. Perhaps he couldn't sleep and went downstairs to get a drink, or something.'

'Perhaps,' Emma nodded. 'But he didn't come upstairs with anything in his hands. One night I got up my courage to peep out. I'd heard him go downstairs, so I looked over the banisters.'

'What was he doing?'

'He was in the hall. Then he went to the front door.' Emma walked her fingers over the duvet cover. 'Really really quietly. I thought he was trying to let someone in,' she shivered, unable to stop herself thinking about the ghosts, despite telling Kate she didn't believe in them. 'But I don't think he was trying to do that.'

'What was he trying to do, then?'

'I think he was trying to get out. He couldn't, because of the new lock Dad put on, but what I want to know is . . .' she turned to Kate, her head held on one side like a curious bird, 'why would he want to go out in his pyjamas at two o'clock in the morning?'

'I don't know, Em. I really don't.'

Kate leaned over and gave her little sister a hug. It was not until that moment that she realised just how much she missed Davey, just how far he had withdrawn from the family.

3

Davey hardly emerged from his room these days – except to eat. At her next opportunity Kate tried to get a good look at him, to see if Lisa was right about his eyes, but she failed. He didn't look up from his plate. When he had finished, he was back up the stairs, using the project as his reason for leaving them. Mum didn't say anything as he excused himself, but Kate could not fail to miss the look her parents exchanged as he left the kitchen.

'Sort out your room while you're up there,' Mum called up the stairs. 'Tom and Ellie are coming for the weekend, so make sure it's tidy.'

'It already is,' Davey shouted back from the landing.

His dad raised an eyebrow, but his mum nodded to confirm that it was true. His sudden tidiness was another worrying sign. Davey's room had been a tip since he was a toddler. They had tried threats and bribes, but nothing worked. Even when Mum had gone in, armed with bin bags and the Hoover to give it a thorough going-over, all the junk just reappeared as if from nowhere, along with the other mess.

No light showed under Davey's door when Kate went to bed. She paused for a second, hand up, ready to knock, but thought better of it. Perhaps he was asleep, and even if he wasn't, what would she say? She thought of the evidence she had accumulated and turned away. You could hardly burst into someone's room and start accusing them of acting strangely, just because they were not talking much and had begun to keep their room tidy.

Kate went into her own room instead and got ready for bed. She lay down with no intention of sleeping. Davey was the one who had premonitions, 'feelings'. He had the 'sight', he knew when things were going to happen, but Kate had her own intuitions. Nothing to do with the supernatural, these were to do with ordinary life and real people. She lay in the dark reviewing the concerns expressed about Davey: by Lisa, her parents, herself and Emma. Taken on their own, they did not add up to very much, but taken together . . .

Kate woke with a start. She must have fallen asleep, despite intending to stay awake. She glanced at the clock radio by her bed. The digital display said: 2:03. She leaned up on one elbow, trying to recall what had woken her up, when she heard it again. A faint pattering, followed by an indistinct shuffling . . .

Kate's heart beat fast and she felt the hairs rising up on her bare arms. Like Emma, she was reminded of the white-faced clown, with his sunken liquid eyes, and little yellow teeth sharp inside the wide red grinning mouth. What if he had come back again? What if he had his hideous comrades with him: the black-draped skeleton and the rubber-faced klansman? There was no reason why it shouldn't happen. Stranger things had, Kate knew for a fact. The clown had got in to the house at Hallowe'en, so why not now? Dad had fitted new locks, but locks and bolts would not bar their way. They were not human.

She looked around the room, eyes wide, alert to any small changes. Sure enough, there was a big bulky shape by the door. That had not been there before. The door was partially opened. It must have slipped in and now she couldn't get out. It was between her and the only exit. Kate kept quite still, her eyes trained on it, ready to detect any little movement. As she watched, it began to sway slightly, as if suddenly aware of her, perhaps alerted by her attention. It was gathering strength, slowly readying itself to come and get her.

It seemed in no hurry. Kate stayed frozen, still balanced on one elbow, half-rising, half-lying, while her heart hammered painfully in her chest and fresh sweat broke out all over. The 'thing' kept up its slow swaying motion, but didn't move any further. Kate forced herself to focus on it and take a good look. It was man-height and wearing a coat, with broad straight shoulders, but no hands. Where the head should be was a little round hook . . .

Kate fell back on the bed, not sure whether to laugh or cry, as relief flooded through her. It was her blazer. The breeze from the open window was causing it to swing about like that. Mum must have collected it from the cleaners and put it on a hanger behind the door. Kate hadn't noticed.

Kate looked at the ceiling, to where twin lights were zipping about. She grinned to herself. Not UFOs, or anything like that. These were old friends. Car headlights climbing the hill.

Just when you think you're safe . . .

Kate sat up again.

There was something moving in the mirror. Her heartbeat instantly returned to its former rapid rate. She had to bite the side of her mouth to stop herself from screaming out. She remembered the mirror in the Room of Ceremonies; it acted as a portal between this world and another. Now, here in her own mirror, in her own room, a ghostly figure was stealing towards her . . .

4

'It's only me.'

Emma turned to the bed, surprised to see her sister with the duvet clutched up to her neck, her eyes all black, wide and terrified, her face white in the moonlight seeping in through a gap in the curtains.

'Who did you think it was?'

'I–I don't know . . .' Kate reached across and pretended to look at the clock, not wanting Emma to see how frightened she was. 'What are you doing in here anyway?' she whispered fiercely. 'It's two o'clock in the morning!'

'I heard Davey get up. I just came to tell you . . .'

Emma hovered uncertainly. Kate had failed to hide her fear. Emma was astonished, and not a little shocked, to find that her big sister could be scared – just like her.

'Where is he now?' Kate scrambled out of bed.

'I–I don't know . . . downstairs I think.' She hesitated. 'You aren't angry with me?'

'No,' Kate managed a smile and ruffled her sister's hair. 'It's just you gave me a bit of a fright. You shouldn't go creeping round people's rooms in the middle of the night.'

'I just wanted you to know about Davey. And I had to be quiet, in case Mum or Dad heard me.'

'Okay, okay. You go back to bed now. I'll go and see what he's up to.'

Kate took Emma back along the landing and then sneaked a look into her brother's room. She could see Davey plainly. His body humped up under the duvet, his dark head resting on the pillow. His face was turned away from her, but he seemed fast asleep. He was not restless in any way and his breathing was deep and regular. Either he had been there all the time, or he had gone back to bed. Kate withdrew quietly, her feelings torn between annoyance and relief. Whichever way, Emma had got her up for nothing.

She stood for a moment, looking over the banister. The stairs were bathed in moonlight, below them was a deep well of shadow. Nothing stirred. Everything was quiet except for the ticking of the hall clock. There was no movement at all, but suddenly her earlier fears came flooding back. Coats huddled round the hat stand like ghosts conspiring, and every gleam of light seemed like eyes looking up at her. The blackness through the glass front door appeared solid, as if the Sentinels were massing . . .

Kate wiped the beads of sweat from her upper lip. She had to get a grip. She was getting worse than Emma. There was nothing down there, she told herself. Nothing! She turned away, getting ready to go back to her own room when a sudden slight shift caught her attention.

There *was* something down there . . .

What she saw scared her far more than any leering white-faced clown or black-robed Sentinel. She drew back instinctively, melting into the shadows, as a figure came gliding into view and began climbing, ascending the stairs on silent feet. It was her brother. But how could that be? Kate put her hand to her mouth to stop herself from crying out. She glanced over to Davey's half-open bedroom door. His form was still under the bed clothes. And yet . . . and yet . . . The figure advanced, walking up the stairs, coming towards her. It was him, but not him. It was his fetch, co-walker, double, *doppelgänger*. The ghostly embodiment of a living human being.

Kate drew back from the banister. Instinct told her not to let it see her. It was like him, but not like. The same height, same size, same clothes, but the face looked narrower, the cheekbones higher. His skin looked white, almost transparent. His short hair stood up like fur over his head. His ears seemed more pointed, set at an odd angle. And his eyes . . .

His eyes were open wide and, in the moonlight streaming down from the window above, they seemed to shine a pale golden amber.

Kate didn't wait to see what happened when the thing went into Davey's room. She crept back to her bed badly frightened, thoroughly spooked. She pulled the duvet round her and then up over her head, blotting out the metallic shafts of moonlight that were coating the room in a weird, unearthly light. She curled herself up in a little ball, her eyes shut tight. She didn't want to see anything else, she just wanted to be inside a cocoon of absolute darkness. Even though the night was still hot, she could not stop shivering and her teeth would not stop chattering.

What was happening to Davey? Kate could not even guess, but one thing she did know – she couldn't handle it on her own. She let up a silent prayer of thanks that Tom and Elinor were coming this weekend. Their visit coincided with the summer solstice. Midsummer. A year to the day since they had gone on the Haunts Ghost Tour and stumbled into the ghost city and this whole thing had started. They planned to go again, this time to say 'goodbye'. The ghosts were leaving the city, and it would be forever.

Kate hoped that they had not already gone. She badly needed help and there was nobody else. Somehow she knew that no one from her world could save Davey now, not even the medium, Mrs Sylvia Craggs.

Time crept on towards morning and gradually Kate relaxed and went to sleep. In her dreams, she journeyed through deserted city streets, setting out to search for the Blind Fiddler, and the highwayman,

Jack Cade, and the others in his ghost crew: Elizabeth, Polly and Govan. She had to find them. Only ghosts would know what was wrong with Davey and how to save him.

5

'What's the matter with you two?' Alison Williams asked when Kate and Davey came down for breakfast. 'You look hag-ridden, the both of you.'

'What does that mean?' Emma asked. 'They've been giving old ladies piggybacks?'

'Something like that,' her mother laughed. 'It's just an expression. It means when you wake up tired for no reason.'

'I didn't sleep very well,' Kate supplied. 'It was too hot.'

'What about you, Davey?' Emma looked over to her brother.

'I slept okay,' he answered, although there were dark smudges under his eyes.

'But you can't stop yawning!'

'Stop bugging me, will you?' He turned on his sister. 'I told you, I slept okay.'

'Wait up, Davey,' Kate said when they were ready to go to school. 'I'll walk with you.'

She was hoping to talk to him, perhaps find out what was wrong with him, but he was halfway out of the door.

'Can't stop,' he shouted over his shoulder. 'I'm meeting Lisa.'

He'd grabbed his bag and was off down the path before Kate could stop him. She went to school with Emma instead. As they walked down the road, Kate mentioned casually about Emma coming to her room, but her sister didn't seem to remember a thing about it. All Kate got was a puzzled look before Emma ran on ahead to meet her friends. Kate let her go. She did not want to alarm her by questioning too closely, and she really was tired, her head full of images from her troubled night. She was having a problem working out what was dream and what was reality. Had she really seen Davey in two places at once? It seemed less and less likely. It seemed like a dream now, like the one where she was searching endlessly, looking for phantoms in the dark moonless streets of a ghost city.

The sunlit suburban road was busy, full of women with buggies, kids going to school, cars pulling out to go to work. Kate drifting along, weaving a way through them all, lost in thought. Suddenly Emma was back by her side, tugging at her bag.

'What is it? What's the matter?' Kate looked down at her sister.

'It's Lisa.'

Kate looked up. 'What about her?'

'Davey said he was going to meet her, but she's there on her own.'

Emma pointed to a small, dark, curly-haired figure, dressed in a white polo shirt and khaki shorts, coming down Puckeridge Rise. Kate sent Emma on ahead, but she waited where the roads met. She wanted a word with Lisa.

'I think you're right,' she said, when the younger girl came up. 'I think there *is* something wrong with him.'

'Any idea what?' Lisa asked as they made their way along the path that led round Derry Hollow and towards the school.

'No,' Kate shook her head. She had decided not to tell Lisa about the *other* Davey since she was no longer sure that she'd seen him herself. If Emma could not remember coming into her room, it meant that she could have dreamt the whole thing. 'But do me a favour,' she added. 'Keep an eye on him at school and report anything strange, anything at all.'

'Sure.'

'Ellie and Tom are coming at the weekend,' Kate added. 'Perhaps Davey'll talk to Tom. Maybe it's a boy thing.'

'Umm, could be,' Lisa nodded, but she did not look completely convinced.

They were nearly at the gates now. Kate looked at her watch. Her school day started before Lisa's did. The Senior bell was about to go any minute.

'I've got to go,' she said. 'I'll meet you here, say quarter to four? See if there's anything more to report. We should be able to get to the bottom of it.'

'I hope so . . .'

'I reckon we can. If we all work together,' Kate said with a smile, trying to reassure herself as well as Lisa.

Lisa sat next to Davey, watching but not watching, keeping an eye out for any strange behaviour, anything she could tell Kate about, but there was nothing. That was the trouble. It wasn't what he was doing, she considered, it was what he wasn't – that's where the strangeness lay. He stared out of the window a lot, but who didn't? On a hot day like this, even their teacher, Mr Craddock, gazed longingly outside, probably dreaming about doing his garden.

When he wasn't looking out of the window, Davey got on with his work. He did nothing to draw attention to himself. He spoke when spoken to. He answered questions, but he joined in none of the chatter and banter that went on when Craddock wasn't looking, or was inclined to let up a bit. Davey was not a swot, or a creep, by any means. He was normally up for most things, but now it was as if he was on autopilot. At break and lunchtime he mooched round by himself. He seemed to sleepwalk through the day.

Davey and Lisa were good friends, best friends in many ways. They had been through a lot together, like that episode at Christmas, with Miss Malkin and the Victorian ghost girl, Elizabeth Hamilton. What had occurred then had been terrifying, but so weird that Lisa sometimes thought that it had not happened at all. They had some-

134

how slipped through time into a different period in the history of the city. They had got caught up in an air raid. Lisa had met her own great-grandfather. They had never discussed what happened, but the strange events had made them even closer.

What he was like now . . . Lisa toyed with her pen, doodling on her rough book. There was a time in the Peace Garden, when it was all over . . . What he was like now reminded her a bit of what he was like then. He had been dazed, stunned by something only he could see and hear. The world around seemed to fade to him; he seemed to be in a different one to her. There was someone he called 'the Lady', someone Miss Malkin was supposed to be. When he spoke of her, his eyes went wide and distant, kind of like they were now.

Lisa risked a sideways look at him. That might account for his expression, but not the change of colour. His deep brown eyes were getting lighter, with a reddish shine in them, almost as if he was wearing colour contact lenses . . .

'What are you staring at?' Davey looked up suddenly, giving her the full benefit of his amber glare.

'You.'

'Well, don't.'

'I just wondered if you were okay.'

'Of course I am.' Davey snapped. 'Why shouldn't I be? Do me a favour, Lisa.' Davey turned his chair so his back was to her. 'Leave me alone.'

Across the table, Billy Hawking went 'ooo-ooh' and

pulled his face into a horrible simper before nudging his neighbour and saying 'lover's tiff' in an exaggerated whisper. Lisa ignored him and got on with her work. When the bell went for the end of the day, Davey stood up from the table and left without saying a word.

'Nothing to report, I'm afraid,' she said when she met Kate.

'Never mind,' Kate shrugged, but she looked disappointed.

'Just one thing . . .'

As they walked along, Lisa explained her theory about Davey and the Lady.

'Does that make any sense?' she asked when she had finished.

'Yes,' Kate replied, sounding a little bit brighter. 'Yes, it just might. Thanks, Lisa.'

'No problem,' Lisa looked up at the older girl and then away again. 'Davey means a lot to me,' she blushed slightly. 'I don't mean in *that* way. I just mean he's a really good friend. I don't know what's wrong with him, but if I can help in any way at all . . .'

'Yeah, I know.'

'He'd do the same for me, if he was acting normal. That's what's odd – he's usually really caring and loyal – and funny,' Lisa paused for a moment. 'I can't remember the last time he cracked a joke, or even smiled.'

'Hmm, that's true.'

Kate couldn't recall the last time herself, come to think of it. Must have been back in May. After they had helped the ghosts to defeat Eugene Hutton, the ghost-hunter. The last time the twins were here. She remembered Davey having a laugh with them. It was round about her birthday. They had gone to the May Day Fair as part of the celebrations. She remembered Tom and Davey had been joking about something on the way there.

'It's little things,' Lisa was saying. 'Today at dinner, for instance. The helpers like Davey – I mean, he's *usually* so cheery. We had semolina. They know he likes it, he's about the only person who does, so they give him more, with an extra dollop of jam as well. Today he didn't even say "thank you", and he hardly touched it. It's only a small thing.' She made a sign with finger and thumb. 'But small things mount up.' She half-turned away, and when she went on her voice was quiet. 'It's as though he doesn't care about anything any more.'

'I know what you mean.' Kate had been thinking the same thing. 'But maybe it's just us. Maybe he needs to see different faces. Tom and Ellie are coming. We plan to go into town tomorrow night.'

'That's a good idea. Take him out of himself a bit.'

'Yeah,' Kate nodded, 'that's what I thought.'

'Well,' Lisa turned to go. 'I hope it works. See you, Kate.'

'Yeah. See you, Lisa.'

Kate watched the younger girl go. Tomorrow night,

they intended to go on another ghost walk. Not one run by Haunts Tours, one of their own devising. It was a long-standing arrangement. The ghosts were leaving the city, and this would be their last chance to see them. Now the ghost walk had added importance. Kate didn't know, any more than Lisa, what was the matter with her brother, but the feeling she had was growing stronger: only the ghosts could help him now.

6

Kate's disturbed sleep from the night before caught up with her and that night she went to bed early. The heat of the day still lingered and light from outside peeped through her curtains, but she went to sleep easily enough.

At first her sleep was deep and dreamless, but gradually she began to surface into a world so real that she could not be completely sure whether she was dreaming or not. She was in the ghost city, just as she had been the night before, and she was searching, looking for somebody, or something, but she did not know what. Maybe she was looking for Davey. Maybe she was looking for someone to help him . . .

She set off down narrow twisting streets, past deserted higgledy-piggledy timber-framed houses louring down at her from under a dull grey-brownish sky. It was not like the times she had been there before. What Kate saw made her increasingly uneasy. The Judge's house, in Fiddler's Court, looked burnt out. The doors and windows were empty spaces, sooty black scorch marks licked up from the shattered casements, staining the grey stone.

All the houses seemed empty. On Quarry Street doors were hanging open. Johnswell's cobbles were littered with torn items of clothing, battered pots and pans, broken crockery. Her uneasiness was rapidly turning into a creeping fear. Jack Cade had said that the ghosts were leaving, but this looked liked a city that had suffered sacking and looting after the population had fled.

She turned the last corner, making for *The Seven Dials*, the inn where Jack Cade and his ghost crew lived. He had told her that they were not leaving until midsummer, and it was not midsummer yet. She stood outside the large timber-framed building. It told that same story. Doors open, windows smashed. The inn sign was hanging off its hinges. It looked like someone had used it for target practice.

Kate turned away in bitter disappointment. There was obviously no one there to help her. She reached Harrow Lane, the old thoroughfare leading out of the city. It was as empty of life as a sepia print. Kate looked up and down, her frustration blooming into panic. If the ghosts had left then who, or what, remained here?

As if on cue, she had a sudden strong feeling of being watched. She looked around, even more fearful. She set off again, starting down the steep stone flight of Keeper's Stairs, increasing her pace as she went. Her initial purpose, her need to search, was swamped by alarm and a desire to escape, for now she had a powerful sense of being followed. It was like the second time she went through the mirror in the Room of Ceremonies, with Davey, when they went after Dr Monckton, the sinister archivist from the city Museum. Then they had been followed by

Govan, but she had the definite feeling that this was not him. The sound was different. Govan's feet had pattered, a barefoot boy steps light across the cobbles. This tread was much heavier: a kind of dragging padding. It had started with one set of footsteps, but now there were more . . . Every time she turned, she saw nothing, but as soon as she set off the following started again.

She ran down past the door into the underground city and on to the end of Keeper's Stairs. From there she turned right at the bottom of the steps. She was in a long road curving up and off to the left.

She could not remember ever being in this street before, either waking or dreaming. The whole area seemed to be in a different time again. It was run-down and decaying, but unmistakably modern. Chinese take-aways and Indian restaurants alternated between small shops. Dirt drifted in litter-strewn doorways. The dusty windows stood empty, the glass smashed, or cracked, or boarded up. There was still no one about. She risked a look behind her. She could see nothing, but the presence there was overwhelming. She could hear them coming on. A sharp, high-pitched note echoed above her, to be answered by another. They were whistling, signalling to each other.

Kate ran as fast as she could, chest heaving for breath, heedless now of where she went. This was as real as any waking life she knew. She had lost all sense that she was dreaming.

The road seemed to disappear beneath her feet, turning into a rough track. She was being chased by a whole pack of them. From behind her came the rhythmic rap of pounding feet, sounding almost like hoofbeats. She rounded a corner and found herself on a ledge. On one side the land sloped up, stones and rock topped by rough grass; on the other, a sheer cliff fell away from her. She was on a bluff overlooking the river. The path finished in a dead end. Her pursuers were close behind now. The only way was up.

Small hovels leaned against a cliff face riddled with caves, hollowed-out dwelling places. She looked in, thinking she might be able to hide, but immediately shrank back. Deep inside, white shapes seemed to move and writhe. She skirted the entrances and began to climb. The path took her past a series of crumbling entrances. Soft worm-like things were issuing from them. A clammy hand fastened itself round her ankle, then another, pulling her down . . .

Suddenly there was a man standing above her. He was holding a sword. He slashed left and right. The white shapes shrank back with a whining, mewing noise and a strong arm reached down to pull her up.

'Well, Mistress Kate, you have led us a fine chase.'

It was Jack Cade. Govan was with him. The boy stood panting, hands on thighs.

'The city stripped of ghosts is a dangerous place for mortals to wander in,' the highwayman said, looking about grimly. 'Other things creep out to take their place. Cave wights, banished spectres, all manner of low and evil creatures. The gutter-sweepings of every century . . .' he glanced round warily and did not sheath his sword. 'Come,' he held out his other hand to her, 'we will be safe up here. The Blind Fiddler is waiting. He sensed you searching, both this night and the night before. He sent us to meet you, but we had no way of knowing where you would enter the city. We did not find you until it was almost too late. He is waiting. Come with me . . .'

He took Kate by the hand and led her up to a grassy expanse at the top of the bluff. The turf was short here, springy underfoot. The Blind Fiddler was sitting on an old stone set in the middle of the green sward. He appeared to be staring straight ahead, his long fingers laced round the top of his staff. Elizabeth and Polly sat at his knee, like grandchild and daughter. Govan ran from Jack's side to be with the old man, settling on his other side like a seeing dog.

Opposite the Fiddler's seat stood a high stone wall. It was built right at the edge of the cliff, looking out across the river. It might once have been part of a castle, or some kind of church, but there was nothing now to show what the building had been. All that remained was a ruin, a curtain of stone, fretted with arches and windows.

The ghosts rose in welcome, making room for Kate to join them.

'Welcome, child.' The Blind Fiddler groped for her

hand. 'I have been waiting for you. I want to know why you search so diligently, even in your dreams.'

'It's about Davey,' Kate drew nearer. 'I'm worried about him. He's, he's been so strange lately. It's not just me,' she added, 'Lisa's noticed, too.'

'Lisa?' He asked and Elizabeth looked up at the name of her kin. 'The girl who helped to save him from the Lady?'

'Yes,' Kate nodded. 'We've both seen a big change in him. Ever since May Day, he's just not been the same.'

'How? How is he changed?'

'He,' Kate paused to think, 'he just doesn't seem to care about anything, or anyone, any more. He spends a lot of time by himself, and at night he wanders about.' Her voice dropped to a whisper as she told him what had happened the night before.

'Hmm, I see.' The Fiddler closed his blind eyes and dropped his head in thought. 'This has happened since Beltane, you say?'

'Beltane?'

'May Day.'

'Yes. He was quite normal before then.'

The Blind Fiddler beckoned Jack and Elizabeth closer to him. The ghost girl and the highwayman approached from where they had been listening.

'Davey was involved in the episode with the ghost-hunter, was he not?'

Jack nodded.

'Could he have been damaged?'

'I think not,' Jack said.

'He *was* affected by the Cleansing,' Elizabeth added. 'But he seemed to recover from it.'

'I do not think it is that,' Jack shook his head. 'I think it is something else entirely.'

'What?'

'Davey was at the Beltane Fair,' the highwayman looked round cautiously. 'Others were there . . .'

'You mean . . .'

'Yes, They were there, the Fair Folk.' Jack Cade dropped his voice. He disliked even talking about them, let alone using their real names. It was a superstitious dread that went back to his country childhood. 'The Lady and some of her band. I do not know what her intentions were, but you can be sure they were not good. I warned you, Kate, did I not?'

'Yes, and we did lose Davey for a while . . .' Kate paused. 'Do you think she might have got to him? Do you think she might be doing this?'

The Fiddler nodded. 'It is possible. More than possible. The Old Grey Man, her father, has forgiven her Midwinter meddling. She is strong between Beltane and Midsummer, it is her time of year. Tomorrow is her day, so we must all be very careful . . .'

'But why should she still want Davey so much?'

'Who knows? She sometimes takes a shine to a mortal, man or child, and if she has set her heart on him, she will not be thwarted.'

'Davey wouldn't go with her,' Kate shook her head. 'He hates her.'

'There are many ways . . .' the Fiddler's fingers brushed the strings of the violin he always carried with him. 'I was not always as you see me. Once I was young, and some thought handsome,' his hand strayed to his head and face, 'with thickly curling red hair, a straight nose and lips ever turned up in a smile, and large bright eyes the colour of robins' eggs. I had travelled far from the land of my birth and found myself here at the time of the Beltane Fair. The Fair was a very great gathering, bringing folk from everywhere, both the living and the dead, from this world and others, but I was just a young fiddle player. I knew nothing of that then.

'As I moved through the fair, delighted by the excitement, my eyes feasting on the sights, I heard the most wonderful air, a divine tune, intricate and lyrical, but wild at the same time, played by a master. I followed the sound, seeking to join him and maybe steal from him, for I earned my living by fiddle and bow. I soon found the player, and others too. I joined them, playing alongside them through the night to the day. It was the most dazzling company. The musicians were the finest I had ever heard, and the dancers! One in particular caught my attention. She was the most beautiful girl I had ever seen. She brought me food and she brought me drink; she showered me with gold.' He paused in his telling. 'I stayed with them, as I thought for just a few days, long enough to dally with her,

146

and learn their tunes and take them away. I would be gone by Midsummer.' He gave a laugh, sharp and bitter. 'By then I would be away. I got away all right, and I took with me their tunes, but that was all. For when I left . . .' His hand shook on the neck of the violin. His voice quavered as if at some deep remembered shock, and tears squeezed from his eyes' closed lids. 'When I left, the world was changed and changed again. I was an old man, condemned to wander without sight. She took my eyes because I had seen what I should not.'

'She?' Jack Cade questioned. 'The beautiful girl, she was . . .'

'The Lady?' The Fiddler finished his sentence. 'Indeed, she was. She took my sight, but she made me a seer,' he pointed to his unseeing sockets, 'because that amused her. I could look into men's hearts, but not their faces. I could gaze into the future, but not at the land, or sea or sky. I can still hear her laughing . . .' He shook his white head. 'That is what happens to those to whom the Lady gives her love. She is beautiful beyond words to describe, but cruel beyond the measure of man. She can turn your eyes to wood, your heart to stone. She can come between you, and all that you hold dear, so that all you want is her. I fear that is what she is doing to Davey.'

'What can we do to save him?' Elizabeth had been listening to the tale with mounting horror. She had known something of the Fiddler's story, but not all. 'How can we help him? We must go tomorrow.'

147

'Kate must bring him here, to the city. We have until the new day dawns to find a way to aid him.'

The Fiddler turned his blind eyes towards the edge of the bluff. The cliff faced east. Across the river, the sky was turning from deep grey-black, becoming lighter, streaked across with long soft ribbons of violet, pink and orange.

'That,' he said, gesturing to the central arch in the wall in front of them. 'That is the Door of No Returning. Tomorrow, as Midsummer dawns, we must pass through.'

The tall pointed archway was directly aligned to the rising sun. As Kate watched, the first pinpoint of light broke through the darkness on the far horizon. The rays radiated out into a luminous halo, filling the doorway with dazzling light, spilling across the green to touch the stone on which the Fiddler sat. It seemed that she could see black shadows outlined against the brilliance, as wave after wave of ghosts passed to the world beyond.

7

Kate woke to the clock radio chattering away on the bedside table. She was back in her own room. The duvet was on the floor and the sheet was twisted around her like a rope. The sun was fully up, pouring in through the gap in the curtains. She felt a momentary panic that she'd be late for school, then realised it was Saturday. Normally she loved that feeling; thinking it was a school day and then realising that it was the weekend, but today it held none of the usual pleasure. She sank back against a pillow still damp with tears of fear and night-time sweat and thought about the dream she'd had. Except it did not seem like a dream. She remembered all of it, for one thing, and she was exhausted. She ached as though she had walked every step.

'Kate?' Her mother's voice came from downstairs. 'Are you up yet? Tom and Ellie will be here any minute.'

Kate looked at the clock. Was that the time? She *had* overslept. The twins were going to be dropped off early. Her aunt and uncle were going away for the weekend. Kate got out of bed and stepped into the shower. She stood under the running water, letting it pour over her, trying to wash away her nightmares.

By the time she was dressed and downstairs, the twins were already there, watching TV in the living-room.

'Hi,' she said as she came into the room. 'Here.'

She gave them a present each. Earrings for Ellie, who had just been allowed to have her ears pierced, and a CD for Tom.

'From Davey and me. Happy birthday.'

The Davey part was not strictly true. Kate had bought and wrapped the presents herself. The twins had hit thirteen on Thursday, two days previously, and Davey had forgotten all about it. They wouldn't even have got a card if Mum hadn't sent one for him. As for a present? Forget about it.

'Cool,' the twins said in unison as they unwrapped their presents. 'Thanks.'

'Where's Davey?' Tom asked. Usually his cousin was first down to meet them.

'He's upstairs, I guess.' Kate put out her hand as Tom got up. 'Wait. Before you go to see him, there's something that you ought to know . . .'

Kate turned up the volume on the TV and told them about Davey. She told them about how Lisa had come to her, and the changes they both saw. She told them about seeing his double on the stairs while he was asleep in bed.

'Are you sure it wasn't a dream?' Tom asked.

'I've thought about that,' Kate replied. 'And I'm pretty sure it wasn't. I tell you, Tom, something *really* strange is happening to him.'

'When was this?'

'Night before last.'

'What about the night just gone?'

'This is not to do with Davey, not directly, but I did have the weirdest dream . . .'

'Astral projection.' Elinor remarked when Kate had finished.

'I beg your pardon?' Her brother raised a sceptical eyebrow, a look he reserved for when he had not heard of something.

'That's what it's called,' his sister explained with a sigh. 'I saw it on a TV programme. Another name is "lucid dreams", like OBEs—'

'Come again?'

'Out of Body Experiences. People are aware that they are in one place, in bed asleep say, but they appear to be in another place, the ghost city, in this case. Although on one level they know that they are dreaming, the experiences they are having feel totally real to them, not like dreams at all.'

Yes,' Kate said, before Tom could interrupt again. 'That's what it was like exactly.'

'Hmm,' Tom remained unconvinced. 'They could still be just dreams. How would you know for certain that you've had one of these OBEs, or whatever?'

'There's only one way to find out,' Elinor replied. 'We go to the city tonight. Go on the ghost walk as planned. If nothing happens, it was just a dream. If not . . .'

She left the sentence unfinished.

151

'Yeah, that's a good idea,' Kate agreed.

'What about Davey?' Tom asked.

'What about him?'

'Should he come with us?'

'What do you mean? The Blind Fiddler said—'

'Ah, but if it *was* just a dream, it might be dangerous for him. Taking him into the lion's den, so to speak. It might even be a trap . . .'

'I see what you mean . . .' Kate frowned, suddenly troubled. She hadn't thought about that.

'What if he doesn't want to go anyway?' Elinor suggested, following her brother's lead. 'It might be better to leave him at home . . .'

'Hmm,' Kate thought for a minute. 'It's been a while since he said anything about it. He might even have forgotten, along with everything else . . .'

'There's one way to find out.' Tom stood up.

'What's that?'

'Ask him what he wants to do. I can stow this at the same time.' Tom picked up his rucksack.

Tom came down, his freckled face pale. His mouth twitched in a slight flinch, and his grey-green eyes were narrowed as if he had recently suffered some kind of blow.

'What's the matter with you?' Elinor asked, alarmed by the obvious pain her twin displayed. 'How's Davey?'

'He – er – invited me to "go away",' Tom replied, trying to smile, trying to make a joke of it. 'Didn't even say "Happy Birthday". One thing you don't have to worry about, though. He won't be going with us tonight. He says he'd rather go to some barbecue.'

'That's where Mum and Dad are going,' Kate explained. 'One of Emma's friend's parents are having a party. We were all invited, but I said we were doing something else. I wouldn't have thought Davey—'

'Whatever.' Tom threw himself down on the settee and concentrated on watching TV. He gradually relaxed, but the hurt expression Ellie saw stayed in place. Although they didn't see each other all the time, Davey and Tom were close – almost like brothers. Davey looked up to Tom, usually they got on really well, so how could Davey treat him like this? She had not yet seen her cousin, but there had to be something very wrong with him. The look on Tom's face convinced her more than anything that Kate could have said.

8

'Are we going on the Haunts Ghost Tour?' Tom asked as they crossed the bridge into the Old Town.

'No,' Kate shook her head. 'I'm not even sure that they do them any more. Anyway, it would be a waste of time. This isn't a nostalgia trip. We are here to find the ghosts before they leave, to see if they can help Davey.' Kate led them down to the river. 'We'll go this way. It's quicker.'

They picked their way past the clearing and building work still going on as part of the Riverside Development Project. Most of the area was fenced off, but a large part of the old riverbank path was still intact. It wound its way round the old docks and wharves; past warehouses and storehouses that now stood gutted, buildings waiting to be restored and remodelled into flats, offices, a new visitors' centre. The old ships' chandlers' was already undergoing conversion into a maritime museum.

Eventually they ran out of pedestrian pathway and had to leave the riverside for the streets behind. This was not an area of the city that Tom and Elinor knew at all. The road that they were following seemed pretty run-down, full of tired, dusty shops, shabby-looking pubs and clubs and low-grade cheap hotels.

It led to a long sweeping section of elevated highway

that roughly followed the line of the river and formed part of the system of bypasses and link roads looping the city. Two modern bridges joined it on either side of a low bluff.

The bluff was cut off now, isolated by the complex of roads designed to keep cars and lorries away from the Old Town. The cliff could only be reached by walking underneath a huge traffic exchange. Kate led them down into a foul-smelling underpass. The tunnel was in need of repair. Pools of unidentified liquid stained the concrete floor. They had to step carefully to avoid pitfalls and places where the yellow graffiti-daubed tiles were flaking off the walls.

The underpass led into a labyrinth of enormous pillars and stanchions that held up the roads circling above. It was dark under there. The far wall was natural rock, the same soft red sandstone Kate had seen last night in her dream. Then the cliff face had been riddled with caves. They were still there. The hovels were still there, too, although they were now constructed from plastic and cardboard. They were occupied. Kate could see eyes gleaming inside and the glow of a small fire. She looked down at the ground. There were bottles and cans littered around. Kate was reminded of the cave wights, the loathsome cave-dwelling creatures that she had encountered the night before.

A man's voice growled, 'Spare some change,' and she jumped.

'Yeah, any change, pet?' a lighter voice chimed and Kate looked down to see a polystyrene cup thrust towards her, gripped by thick grime-seamed fingers and black and broken nails. Little dark eyes looked out of a mass of matted, straggly hair. A big beard, stained round the mouth, bushed like a cloud of wire wool from underneath a sheeny purple-grey nose.

'How about you? The little ging'er?'

The man next to him leered up at Elinor. He was younger, not much more than a boy. His skin was pale, pimpled and marked by bad nutrition. He took a swig from his beer can and leered again, showing yellow uneven teeth.

Kate was not sure what to do. Tom and Elinor drew nearer to her. All three of them stood staring at the two men until the unmistakable sound of a mobile phone broke into the tense silence growing between them. Kate's hand groped for her pocket. The young man's grin grew wider. Mum had got the phone after the last time they all came back late from the city . . .

'Here you are, mate.' Tom dug into his pocket and threw all the change he had before grabbing Kate, who was staring like a mesmerised rabbit. 'Come on,' he hissed. 'Let's get out of here!'

They ran for stairs that led up to an island surrounded by the whine and drone of traffic. The phone was still trilling. At the top, Tom hung over the steps to see if the men were following. The younger of the two had, indeed, shambled to his feet, but when he saw where they were heading, he hesitated and then went back. Tom leaned back, breathing a sigh of relief that the young tramp could not be bothered to climb all the way up to them.

Kate turned away from the traffic noise to answer the call.

'Sorry,' she said. 'It went off when we were in the middle of the road—

'—Do I? We were running—

'—Oh, right. Okay, then—

'—Er, yes. No. Not right now. He's, he's, um, gone off with Tom somewhere—

—Yes. Yes. We'll try. See you later. Yes. Bye.'

She put the phone back in her pocket.

'It's okay,' Tom said to her, jerking his thumb towards the stairs. 'I don't think they can be bothered.' He nodded towards the phone. 'I didn't know you had one of those.'

'Mum bought it after the last time when we all got separated.'

'Was that her?' Elinor asked, alerted by the sick look on Kate's face.

Kate nodded.

'What did she want?'

'She phoned to say that Emma is staying over, so they would be back late.'

'That's all right,' Tom said. 'It gives us more time.'

'That's not all she said.'

'What else?' Elinor came over to her cousin and took her arm. 'Is it about Davey?'

'Yes . . .' Kate bit her lip. 'He's not with them. He's supposed to be, but he's not. She thinks he's with us.'

'And you told her he was with Tom – why didn't you tell her the truth?'

'Because I didn't want to worry her – and it wouldn't make any difference.'

'Try the phone. See if he's at home.'

Kate did as Tom said. There was no reply.

'Where is he?'

Kate sat down on a concrete seat with no back. 'Goodness knows.'

'What are we going to do?'

'Wait here, I suppose.'

Tom and Elinor looked about. The top of the bluff was not much like the vibrant close-cropped green Kate had described from her dream. The wide oval space was choked with car-thrown, wind-blown litter: cans and wrappers, brown paper bags and polystyrene food containers. A few weeds showed here and there, rank yellow flowers, straggling along the path or struggling through long grass, tough and thick, stiff with grey dust and black grit.

'Is this it?' Elinor frowned and Tom looked doubtful.

Kate nodded. This was the right place. The big squat boulder where the Blind Fiddler had been sitting was still there, although almost covered now by a swirling stook of seeding grass. Opposite to it, on the far side, stood the curtain of stone. It looked thinner, more eroded, as frail as lace against the deepening midsummer blue.

'We'll just have to wait,' Kate said. 'Wait for the ghosts to come. They are the only ones who can help us now.'

9

Davey lay on his bed, resting on a cat's cradle of lies. He had never dreamed it would be so simple. First he had told Kate that he did not want to go into the city. He was going with Mum and Dad and Emma to the barbecue party. Kate had not kicked up the kind of fuss he'd thought she would, which was good. She had gone off with Tom and Elinor to get the bus and go on the ghost walk. Then, at the last minute, he'd told Mum and Dad that he'd changed his mind, that he wanted to go to the city after all. He'd left the house, supposedly to follow his sister and cousins, but really he'd doubled back, waited for his parents to leave the house, and then nipped in through the back door.

He had slipped between them. In trying to catch him, they had all missed. He laced his fingers behind his head and stared up at the ceiling with a small smile of satisfaction. Easy.

He lay quietly, watching the changing light from outside slide over the walls. He sought no other amusement. His stereo and TV were silent, the computer screen blank. The games CDs stood neatly stacked, gathering dust. He had no need for them any more. Soon it would be time. Soon.

Downstairs the phone rang and rang, but he took no notice. He kneeled up on the bed, chin on the window-sill, looking out across the tops of the houses to the wild expanse of Wesson Heath. Beyond that, lay the dark green splodges of Kingswood's undulating forest. Haze-filled valleys and tree-serrated ridges stretched ever onwards to the far horizon, suggesting a timeless, mythical landscape, untouched by man's activity. That was where he wanted to be. Away from all human interference. Free and clear.

The dark blue sky was bleeding crimson and orange at the edges, as if lit from below by unseen fires. It seemed that he could see the curvature of the world. Above it all, the midsummer sun hung midway from heaven, falling towards the west like a bloody red ball.

10

Elinor was scared. She did not like this place. She was afraid those men might come up after them, but Kate would not hear of going. This was where she had arranged to meet the Blind Fiddler and here she would stay – all night if necessary.

'You can go if you want to,' she said, knowing that they wouldn't leave her.

'But what about those men?'

'They will not come up here, Elinor,' someone said behind her. 'Never fear.' She turned to see the highwayman, Jack Cade. He winked and smiled down at her. 'They think that this place is haunted.'

'Jack!' Kate jumped up. 'Where are the others?'

'They are here.'

She looked around to see Polly and Elizabeth. Standing with them was the Blind Fiddler, his hands resting on Govan's shoulders.

'I didn't hear you.'

Jack's grin widened, and his dark eyes sparkled. 'Of course not. We are ghosts.' He swept off his hat to them all. 'Kate, Tom, Elinor – how do you do? And where is Davey?'

As Kate explained, he became suddenly grave. He

listened carefully, not interrupting, turning his hat round in his hands. The others gathered to hear what she was saying. Kate looked from one ghost to the other. They all stared back, their eyes sombre and anxious.

'It is as I feared,' the Fiddler said when she had finished. 'The Lady works to thwart our best endeavours.'

'The Lady?' Elinor looked at him, eyes widening.

'Certainly.'

'But surely, she is nowhere near Davey. I thought that her place was here . . .' Elinor looked out over the bluff, past the circling traffic, towards the Old Town.

'That is just *one* of her places,' the old man corrected her. 'She has many. Another of her places is Dwerry Hollow, as you discovered at Hallowe'en.'

He used the old name: 'Dwerry' meant dwarf, or changeling. Elinor turned away with a shudder, clutching her arms to her. The present evening still held the heat of the day, but she was suddenly wrapped in the freezing temperatures of Derry House's basement, with the fairy woman's silver eyes staring down into hers.

'So she *could* be at Derry Hollow . . .' Kate said, her mind struggling to take in the implications. 'What about the rest of them? The Host, the Unseelie Court?

The Fiddler shrugged his slightly stooped shoulders. 'All I can say for certain is that they are not here. Their Knowe is empty. I have just come from there. They have either moved to other lodgings or—'

'Or what?' Jack Cade asked, impatiently.

'This year a great Hosting is taking place far to the west. They may have set off for it already, or they may have stopped on their way—'

'To pick up a passenger, as it were.' Tom finished his train of thought.

'Indeed, Thomas.'

'We have to get to him!'

Kate jumped up, frantic. Home. The very place where they thought that Davey would be safe had turned out to hold the greatest danger of all. Derry Hollow was about a hundred metres from their house.

'Wait, Kate! It's no use just racing off. We need to know more before we do that. I don't understand,' Tom turned to the Blind Fiddler. 'What does she want with Davey, anyway?'

'She is working some deep enchantment, just as she did at midwinter. That time she failed, but she learns from her mistakes. Now she baits her trap with sweetness. She has entered into him, poisoning from within, turning his heart to stone, so he no longer cares for the things of this world. Once the process is complete, it will be impossible to save him. He will be lost forever.'

'How so, Blind Fiddler?' Elizabeth's grey eyes widened with fear for her human friend. 'How so?'

'Before, she sought to capture him. Now he goes of his own free will. Once he is in her power, he will be lost.'

'But how?' Elizabeth's black brows drew together. 'I still do not see . . .'

'Because he will want to stay with her. He will see no reason to return.'

'But what about us?' Kate interjected. 'His family, his friends . . .'

'He will care nothing for you, don't you understand?' The Fiddler shook his head. 'A heart of stone cannot love. He will care nothing for you, or anyone.'

'That – that's awful!' Elinor exclaimed. 'Davey's warm, and considerate. He's – he's generous, and – and affectionate . . .'

Her voice faltered as she took in the enormity of the threat to him. Elinor hated the Lady. Out of everything and everyone that they had encountered since all this started, she feared her most. What she was doing now to Davey was worse than anything Elinor could imagine.

'The enchantment works like their arrows, their elf bolts,' the Fiddler went on. 'If any part remains, the poison will be in him still. He will be *in* this world but not *of* it. He will go through his whole life with a stone where his heart should be . . .'

'You mean he will never love anyone? Ever?'

'That is it exactly.'

'That's – that's terrible. It's evil!'

'Indeed, Elinor,' the Fiddler nodded. 'Indeed it is. You speak more truly than you know.'

'Why are we all standing here *talking*!' Kate exclaimed. 'We've got to find him!' She stared wildly at the circling traffic. 'We ought to get going before it is too late!'

165

'I'm with you, Mistress Kate,' Jack looked at her. 'Go by any means you may. I will go, too. I can travel more swiftly than you.' He smiled, trying to reassure her. 'I will find him, and I will save him, never fear.'

'And if he is already with the Lady?' Kate asked.

Jack drew his sword. 'She will taste this. Her and her company.'

'No,' the Blind Fiddler flinched at the sound of the blade cutting through the air. 'Your weapon will do more harm than good. Do you not listen? The enchantment must be unwoven, not slashed into pieces.'

'How? How can it be done?'

The Fiddler did not answer straight away. He leaned his clasped hands on the top of his staff and bent his head, turning his sight inwards.

'I cannot see clearly.' He raised his eyes in questing enquiry. 'But you must go and you must take Elizabeth.'

'Why me, Fiddler?' the ghost girl whispered.

'I do not know,' the old man heaved his shoulders, 'I just feel that it is so . . .'

'If I cannot use this,' Jack interrupted, sheathing his sword, 'what am I to do?'

'You will find other ways. Other allies.'

'You speak in riddles, old man,' Jack grimaced. 'You are as bad as *them*.'

'Hush, Jack,' Polly hurried forward. 'He is Davey's only hope. Do as he says.'

'Yes, Jack,' Elizabeth threw her long hair back. 'Why do we delay?'

'Come, then,' Jack held out his gloved hand to her. Dell, his black mare, was tethered below.

'Go well, Jack Cade,' the old man held up his hand in blessing. 'Stay well.'

'You, too. Fiddler. Look after Govan and my Polly.'

'Jack! Elizabeth!' Polly called after them. 'Remember you must be back by first light of dawn!'

Elizabeth nodded to show she understood. Jack just smiled and touched the brim of his hat in a gesture of goodbye. When they had gone, Polly turned her face to hide her sorrow, knowing that she might never see either of them again.

11

Davey stared out of the window watching the great red ball of the sun, split by grey spindrift cloud, stain the whole western sky and sink towards the horizon. Soon it would be time to leave for Derry Hollow.

When only the top of the sun showed like a crimson dome, he stood up and went towards the door as if heeding a distant call.

He left his room without a backward glance. He went down the stairs without turning to see the family photos smiling down at him: grandparents, parents, Davey himself, with Kate, with Emma, all three of them together. He did not as much as glance at the people who meant the most to him, even though he might never see any of them again.

He let himself out of the front door, shutting it carefully behind him, went up the path and turned right into the street. Not once did he look back.

He went on down the road, always downwards, heading for Derry Hollow. The lights were coming on in the houses. TV sets flickered in front rooms; barbecue smoke wafted over from back gardens. Street toys lay abandoned on drives and lawns, left as their owners went in for the night. Davey strode on, leaving behind the everyday trappings of suburban life.

When he reached Derry Hollow, he stopped. There was no one around. No one was watching him. He took one last look at the place he had lived all his life and followed the sloping ground down towards Derry House.

Davey was wrong. There *was* someone watching. Higher up the hill, on the other side of the Hollow, Lisa was staring out of her bedroom window. She had been watching the sunset, too. Her room was at the top of a block of maisonettes in Garden Court, high up on Puckeridge Rise, and she had a fine view out over Wesson Heath and beyond.

She saw Davey immediately as he came out of Derry Way at the bottom of the cul-de-sac. She watched him stop and gaze around, and wondered where he could be going at this time of night. She looked beyond him, thinking to see Kate and the twins, knowing that they were coming for the week-end, but Davey was alone. There was no sign of anyone else. That did not square with what she knew of Kate's plans. Lisa felt mystery begin to surround his sudden appearance.

Davey did not stay in one place long. He set off down the slope towards Derry House. Lisa got up from her seat, craning for a better look. This was even more unexpected.

She did not know exactly what had happened in there last Hallowe'en, but she knew that something had. Davey avoided the place like the plague after that but then, Lisa shivered as goosebumps suddenly furred her arms, didn't everybody?

Now she *knew* there was definitely something strange going on. He was strolling down towards the hulking Victorian house as if he was off to a party.

'I'm just off out, Mum,' she called, grabbing her jacket as she passed the living-room door.

'Where are you going?' Her mum called back.

'See a friend, I won't be long.'

Lisa let herself out through the side door, running down the steps and off down the road into the Hollow.

Derry House driveway was full of skips. She made her way past shards of rotting wood and spilling plaster, walking round the outside of the house. There was no sign of Davey anywhere about.

She went back to her starting point and stopped for a moment to listen. From somewhere came distant music, but it could have been coming from anywhere on the estate, or even up in the village. The Hollow collected sounds into it, like a natural bowl. Lisa stared up at the house. The doors and the ground-floor windows were boarded. The building had been completely stripped out. You could see sky through the roof beams, joists through the frameless upper-storey windows. Davey could not possibly be inside it. The house had no floors. So where had he gone?

She took one last look at the empty house and headed out on to Wesson Heath.

12

Davey went down into the Hollow, following the drive towards the back of Derry House. As he entered the part in deepest shadow, he saw a man coming towards him. At first, he thought it must be the Blind Fiddler, but though white-haired, this man walked straight, with seeing eyes; he had no need for staff or guide.

'Who are you?' Davey asked, although he already knew the answer.

'You know who I am,' the man's voice had a deep, ringing quality and the words came slowly, as though he was unused to human speech. 'I am the Old Grey Man.'

The leader of the Host. The King of the Unseelie Court. He stood tall, towering over the boy. Davey looked up into a face that was very far from human. His eyes were large, almond-shaped, set wide, stretching almost to the sides of his head. Davey could see no white; pupil and iris were silver. Bones showed clearly beneath skin the colour of pewter. Great age showed in the fine lines mapping his face and his beard was long. The flowing mass of his hair was the colour and texture of spiders' webs.

'Come.' He offered Davey an impossibly thin, long-fingered hand. 'My daughter is eager to see you. We must not keep her waiting.'

Davey glanced round, suddenly aware of someone else, standing close by the house. As he went towards her, she stepped out.

Davey had always considered the Lady to be beautiful, but now she appeared far, far more than that. She had discarded any pretence of human disguise and was as she is. Her gown was of the finest material, white and shimmering, shot through with silver and gold. Her long fair hair, the colour of ripened wheat, flowed into the folds. Her eyebrows swept up, angled above large, wide, slanting eyes that were the translucent green of emeralds. High cheekbones and a pointed chin accentuated the hollows in her face. Her wide mouth curved back in a smile, showing small white teeth.

'Welcome, Davey.' She held out her hand to him. Her skin was as smooth as fine white porcelain, absolutely unlined, but her eyes were as deep as the deepest ocean, the expression within them as old as time. 'Welcome to my home. Enter freely.'

'Thank you.' Davey stepped towards her, his own eyes circles of pale clear amber. 'Thank you, I will.'

The earth seemed to crack wide for them to go inside. Music floated up from the interior, the most wonderful music Davey had ever heard. The sound mingled with wild high cries, the excited calls he remembered from the May Day Fair. Davey quickened his step. It meant *those*

173

people were there. The Lady put her arm around his shoulder as she led him down the gentle slope and into the fairy knowe.

'They are all waiting for you. It is your home now.'

Davey went gladly. This seemed so right. It felt as though he had been waiting for this moment since before the beginning of his life. Over his head, the Lady smiled at her father. The Old Grey Man smiled back at her. He did not understand why she had set her heart on this human boy, but she was his beloved daughter, he could deny her nothing. The Old Grey Man looked down at the child walking between them. As soon as the earth closed behind them, this boy would forget that he had ever known any other life.

13

Jack Cade rode with Elizabeth, taking Harrow Lane down to the river. From here he took the footbridge across to what remained of the old roads: back streets and twisting cobbled alleys; parts of dual carriageway; footpaths through bleak industrial estates and high-rise housing developments. He went through the city's outskirts and into suburbs that once had been ploughland, woodland, fields and meadows. All along the way stood stones, old posts and crosses, some lost, some removed, some still there but weed-choked and long-neglected, placed to mark the old track that led to Wesson Heath.

No one saw him, but a few people shivered and looked up to see if the sun was clouding. Here and there, dogs barked. Cats bristled, hissing at nothing. Horses shied, scattering from their grazing as he passed by.

Nothing could impede a ghost horse and riders. They made good progress. Better progress than Kate, Tom and Elinor. They left Polly with the Blind Fiddler and Govan and slogged their way through underpasses and overpasses up to the new road interchange. From there they took one of the new motorway bridges across the river.

The wide road did not make pleasant walking. Three

lanes of cars and lorries streamed in either direction. The noise was constant. Dust made their eyes sore and gritty; their throats and noses felt choked, blocked with exhaust fumes.

Once they were over the river, Kate found the right bus stop, but they had to wait for what seemed like ages for a bus to come along. Then, when they were on, it seemed to stop at every possible stop. Kate scowled at the slow snake of passengers shuffling on and off and stared out of the window in an agony of impatience.

'I've known speedier *snails*,' Tom whispered as the bus lumbered and juddered through the traffic.

The streets were full, the pavements crowded. The warm June evening had brought everybody out. Time was getting on. Neon showed from cafés and restaurants. Light spilled from pubs and late-opening shops.

'Come on! Come on!' Kate sat forward in her seat, urging the bus on, just as she had done as a small child.

'What are we going to do when we get there?' Elinor asked. 'See if he's at your house?'

'No,' Kate grimaced. 'There's no point. He's not going to be sitting there waiting for us, is he?'

'Where will he be, then?'

'I don't know. It's up to us to find him.'

'But how can we? Perhaps we'd better go and find Auntie Alison and Uncle Stephen . . .'

'And tell them what?' Kate turned on her cousin, blue

176

eyes blazing. 'It's gone too far for that. They wouldn't listen to us, you know what adults are like. They might *say* Davey's away with the fairies, but I don't think they know how close to the truth that is. They might even call the police, and would *they* listen? It would just mean a massive big fuss and we *still* wouldn't get him back.'

Elinor wasn't sure. She looked at her brother.

'What do you think, Tom?'

'I'm with Kate. We've got to do this on our own and hope we can get to him before anyone realises that he is missing.'

'How do we do that?'

'I don't know,' her brother shrugged. 'Wait for inspiration to strike, I suppose. I wish Davey was here . . .' he added and then grinned at what he'd said. 'Well, he *is* the one who has feelings and intuitions—'

'And if we're going to find him, we're going to have to think like him. You're a genius, Tom! Come on,' Kate stood up and reached for the buzzer above her head.

'But we're not there yet!'

'I know, but Wesson Heath's the next stop.'

'I don't recognise it.'

Elinor looked out of the window, frowning. The bus was speeding up, the stops were getting less frequent. The road they were on crossed a little patch of country, a gap between the suburbs, a green space that had yet to be erased.

'Me neither,' Tom agreed. 'I thought it wasn't for ages.'

'This is Wesson Heath Common, not the village.' Kate stood poised as the bus doors wheezed open. 'And this is where we are getting off.'

14

The evening was still warm. Lisa tied her jacket round her waist and followed the same route that Davey had taken at Hallowe'en: across the field, over Gilmore Bridge, along Shaker's Lane and on to Wesson Heath.

Shaker's Lane sloped down into the Hollow Road; a road so old it seemed to have been worn down into the land. Heathland rose up on either side, unfenced, uncultivated. There were no neat hedges here, only patches of gorse and scrub. The few trees were gnarled and bent. Lisa came to a twisted old oak, dwarfed by the wind. Here the way forked. One path led to a green way, unnamed and unpaved, an ancient foot-trodden path passing through a shallow valley and on to the westward expanse of Wesson Heath. The Heath had once covered a much bigger area, spreading wild and open for many miles, before merging into the King's Wood, which had been part of a great forest extending far to the west and south.

The other road led up to Whitestone Hill, the highest point on the Heath. Lisa followed this route, almost without thinking. Even though it was a fine evening, she didn't see any people about. No one came here much, except in the winter to toboggan or for Sunday afternoon rambles, or to walk their dogs. At the top of the hill, this road met three others. The crossroads made a good vantage point. An excellent place to look out for Davey. The summit was marked by the Whitestone, a dirty quartz boulder that lay beside the four roads. Lisa stood on this, shading her eyes.

The setting sun struck across the heath, kindling the gorse to fire, bathing everything in a strange red light. Lisa squinted hard but the glare made it difficult to see a thing.

There was no sign of Davey. It was as if he had vanished into the ground. She got down from the Whitestone and sat on it, chin resting on her hands, wondering what to do.

Far across the heath, Jack's sharp eyes caught the shape of a child sitting on the stone.

'There! Over there!'

He turned Dell's head and made for the Whitestone. At Hallowe'en he'd found Davey waiting at the crossroads.

Elizabeth looked out from behind him, peering over his shoulder. As Dell drew nearer, she could see that the child was a girl, not a boy. Although they were dressed in similar ways, in short-sleeved jersey shirt and coarse blue cotton trousers, the figure was slighter, the hair longer and much curlier.

'It's not him,' she said to Jack.

Jack reined Dell in, set to wheel her back to the path that would take them to Derry Hollow.

'Wait,' Elizabeth gripped his shoulder. 'It is his friend, Lisa. The child who saved him at Midwinter. She is kin to me . . .' Elizabeth paused. 'I sense a certain symmetry. What did the Fiddler say? You will find other allies, other ways? She may have a part to play.'

'There is sense in what you say.' Jack thought it over. 'And we have no other ideas. Night draws on.' The sky above was turning an ever-deeper blue and over towards the west it was a mass of red. He spurred his horse on. 'Let us see if you are right.'

15

Tom and Elinor followed Kate up on to Wesson Heath, although they were both sure that they had got off at the wrong stop.

The sun was going down, slanting red rays across the rough country, making it hard to see anything. Different paths snaked away in different directions. They were not sure where they were going, so did not know which one to take. On a map, the area looked small, but they were on foot, without even a bike between them. They were also tired from their tramp through the city. Wesson Heath spread out all around them and seemed vast.

'Which way?' Tom asked.

Kate shook her head. None of them was blessed with Davey's sixth sense. Now they were up here, the guiding intuition, which had said to get off the bus, seemed to have tuned itself out.

Tom looked around, eyeing the rising ground.

'Let's make for the middle,' he pointed up towards Whitestone Hill. 'From up there, we can see where we are. We can have a good look round as we go, and then, if we don't find anything, we can make for home.'

'We ought to look in Derry Hollow . . .' Elinor added, although this was the last place she felt like going.

'Yes,' Tom agreed. 'We should. Come on, then. Time's wasting.'

The distance did not seem so far, once they had an objective in view. Kate was all for setting off across country, but Tom said that was not a good idea. It might *seem* the quickest way, but the ground in between might be rougher than it looked, with hidden dips, impassable scrub and boggy places. So they stuck to the old road that still traversed the common. It was much easier to walk on its metalled surface, even if it was full of potholes and the unkerbed verges were eroded and broken.

The road undulated over the countryside. Tom looked up as they reached the last rise. The crossroads seemed to be occupied.

Lisa started with surprise. She had been so far into her thoughts and dreams she might as well have been asleep. She had heard nothing. No sound had roused her, no hoofbeats drumming on the road, coming nearer and nearer. She sensed, rather than knew, that someone, or something, was suddenly there, standing right behind her. Her grey eyes widened and her heart jumped up into her throat as she turned and looked up into the froth-flecked, blood-rimmed nostrils of an enormous horse.

The animal stood huge above her. It tossed its head, sweat showing on the rippled muscles of its great black neck. This could not be happening. Lisa closed her eyes and opened them again. She must still be dreaming. The horse was bad enough, but between its twitching ears she could see a highwayman looking down at her, complete with mask and velvet jacket.

Her first instinct was to run, but her legs seemed to have frozen under her. All she could do was stare.

'It's all right, Lisa,' a voice said at her side. 'Don't be alarmed. Do you remember me?'

Lisa nodded. It was Elizabeth Hamilton, the ghost of her great-great-aunt. In looks they were almost identical. The same grey eyes, set wide in a heart-shaped face. The same strong black brows meeting above a straight slightly snubbed nose, and the same full mouth above a chin with a slight cleft.

'Don't be afraid of Jack,' Elizabeth said, and the high-wayman smiled and swept off his hat. 'Or Dell.' The horse neighed at the sound of her name and tossed her black mane. 'They are friends of Davey. We are worried about him, just as I know you are, and we've come here to look for him.'

'Me, too.'

'How so?' Elizabeth's brows drew together in enquiry.

'I thought he was going with Kate and his cousins into town, but then I saw him going down into the Hollow, into the grounds of Derry House.' Lisa shrugged. 'I wondered what he was doing, so I followed him.'

'But he wasn't there?'

'No,' she shrugged again and spread her hands. 'It was as if the earth had swallowed him up . . .'

184

'You speak more truthfully than you know . . .' the highwayman remarked gloomily. He had dismounted now and was standing beside her, his arms folded.

'Shh,' Elizabeth scowled at him. 'Quiet, Jack! Go on, Lisa.'

'There's not much more to tell. I thought he might have come up here, so I wandered up to have a look but there's no sign of him.'

'Hmm.' Jack took a moment to consider, his chin resting on his gloved fist. 'And you have seen nothing since you came up here? Nothing, shall we say, unusual?'

'No,' Lisa shook her head. 'Nothing at all. The place seems quite deserted.'

'Or heard anything?'

'No . . .' Lisa shook her head again. 'Although – wait a minute! I *did* hear something. Kind of distant music . . .'

'What kind of music?'

'Old-fashioned, but not classical. You know, with fiddles and flutes, kind of folk or Irish, something like that.'

'Where did you hear this?' Jack asked.

'Down in Derry Hollow.'

Jack looked at Elizabeth who nodded. 'That sounds like them,' she said.

'Like who?'

'Do you remember the Lady?'

Lisa nodded, thinking of the creature who had taken the shape of Miss Malkin. Lisa had never seen the Lady, except as the teacher, but had experienced the power she could wield; warping time, twisting fate. Just before Christmas she had done just that, nearly destroying Davey and Lisa herself.

'Well,' Elizabeth looked at her. They appeared to be about the same age, but the girl standing here was her great-grand-niece. 'We think that she has taken Davey and this time she means to keep him.'

'But how? Davey would never stay. He will try to escape, put up a fight—'

'Not this time,' Elizabeth shook her head. 'The Lady is subtle, full of cunning and cleverness. She learns from her mistakes. She seems to have worked some kind of enchantment, so he goes to her willingly. She has been preparing him. She must have got to him at some point without anyone realising and planted the spell like poison in his mind. Now he *wants* to be one of them, which makes everything much more difficult than if she had taken him by force.'

'Them? You mean there's more . . .'

'Oh, yes. Scores. Hundreds very probably. They are the Sidhe. The Unseelie Court.'

'And Davey wants to be with them?'

'So it seems.'

It sounded as if the Lady had kind of brainwashed him. Of course! That would account for his strange behaviour. Lisa suddenly understood.

'He hasn't been the same since he went to that fair at

186

May Day,' she said. 'He came back raving about some ride he'd been on, and the people he'd met. The way he went on about them, I thought he'd met a pop star or something . . .'

'That was when it must have happened. I warned Kate that they were about . . .' Jack Cade's face darkened with anger, more at himself than anybody else. He pounded one gloved hand into the palm of the other.

'It's no good blaming yourself, Jack,' Elizabeth laid a hand on his arm. 'We just have to decide what to do now.'

'We can't take the Hollow. We would not even be able to get in. We have not the magic. The Old Grey Man will be there in person. Even the Fiddler would not gain entry without his permission.'

'So what do we do?'

'Wait for them to come out.' Jack looked out over Wesson Heath. 'Tonight is Midsummer. They will ride. The Fiddler said they are hosting far to the west. They will not leave it much after sunset. We can guess the route they will take.'

'How?' Lisa asked.

'Their horses are unshod. They will keep to the old green ways and grass roads and they will be heading west to the setting sun. We will lie in wait. The best place will be where two ways cross. I know just the spot. The whole Host will be there. All the Unseelie Court. They will come by in a long cavalcade led by the Old Grey Man and his daughter. Davey will probably be just behind them. When he rides by, we will seize him.'

'What if we don't manage it?' Lisa's grey eyes narrowed. It seemed like a tall order to her.

'If we do not, they will enter the King's Wood. It will be much more difficult for us to take him once he enters there.'

'So what if we can't do that, either?'

'After the King's Wood, the Host will take to the air. If that happens Davey will be lost forever. You will never see him again.'

16

Jack knew Wesson Heath like he knew his own hand. He led them down one bumpy furze-lined track, and on to another. Every now and then, he lifted his head to scan the horizon. Once or twice he whistled through his white teeth, a single sharp and piercing note.

'What do you look for?' Elizabeth asked. 'The Unseelie Court?'

'No,' Jack gave a grim smile. 'They will not come yet.'

'Who do you call?'

'One who might be of assistance. What did the Fiddler say? You will find other allies, other ways?' He quoted her words back to her. 'Thank you for reminding me, Elizabeth.'

They came to a point where four paths met. Another twisted tree grew here, an old thorn with no leaves and the branches bent up, like fingers clawing the sky. A huge patch of brambles tangled around it, almost covering a crumbling stump of stone that stood at its base. This was all that remained of the Mile Cross, an ancient signpost that marked the meeting of ancient boundaries, and a parting of the ways. To the south lay the village. To the north lay more open heathland. East was the way they had come. A broad green path led west, wide enough to take horsemen riding four abreast. That way led into the dark forest depths and was all set around with ferns. The turf there was soft and springy, velvet as a lawn.

'This is the place!' Jack tethered Dell to the thorn and pointed to the patch of bramble and briar. 'Hide yourselves!'

'How long do we have to wait?' Lisa whispered, briar thorns grabbing at her arms, tangling in her hair.

Lisa slipped her jacket on. The sun had gone from the west and, although it was a warm night, a chill white mist was sneaking up the sunken road from the south, spreading out like thin gauze.

'Not long, I think, Ssh,' Jack put a finger to his lips. 'Do you hear it?'

Lisa listened. At first she heard nothing, then came the ching, ching, chinking ring of many small bells, followed by the soft thud and pad of unshod hooves. The rhythmic ring and silvery jingle jangle of bridle bells was accompanied by wild high laughter that did not sound human. Strange, eerie cries echoed, like birds calling to each other in the gathering darkness. The Fairy Court was abroad.

Lisa knew what they were but, until now, her imagination had furnished their appearance. Her eyes widened in awe as she saw the beings, who were winding their way up the path towards her. These were nothing like the creatures she had created in her mind from films and toys and fairy tales.

They were as tall as humans, slenderly built, pale in the half light, with high cheekbones and slanting eyes. Their long hair flowed as they rode, glowing like burning sheaves of silver and gold. Lisa caught her breath and held it. They were beautiful!

Two columns came towards her, riding one after another. The first were clad in grey, mounted on black horses. Short-bladed swords hung from the riders' belts. Some had quivers of arrows and small deeply curved bows slung across their shoulders. Others carried long lances tipped by silver leaf-shaped blades.

Behind his guard came the Old Grey Man, grey-haired, grey-bearded, grey-gowned, wearing a simple silver crown. He was riding a fine steed, dappled like dull beaten steel, richly caparisoned in silk and lace as fine as cobwebs.

The following troop rode on chestnut bays. Their clothes were paler, silver-bright, and they seemed younger, wilder, laughing and joking with each other, enjoying the cavalcade. They were armed, as before, with lance, bow and sword.

This was the Lady's own guard, her personal band. Behind them she came, riding on a horse of dazzling whiteness, her silver bridle trailing silk. She looked very young, and very beautiful, as she joked with those nearest to her, shaking her silver hair so it streamed behind her, glittering like moonlight on a river. She was smiling and laughing, her slanting eyes gleaming green beneath a pale circlet of gold. Her long gown draped down, flowing in folds, shimmering to matched the shifting change in her eyes, from silver to green and back again.

Behind her came another milk-white steed, smaller than hers, little bigger than a pony. On it rode Davey. But how he was changed! Lisa gasped, her eyes wide with wonder. He had become one of them! He was dressed like the rest in grey and silver. His features had taken on a fine chiselled cast and his eyes gleamed pale amber. His dark hair clung to his head, sleek as fur, and a gold star shone on his brow.

The Lady turned to gaze back at him, her silver eyes gleaming with pride and hard-won possession. Then the column broke. The first group, with her in it, wheeled to take the curving turn in the road that would lead them to the west. Their bridle bells jingled, and their pace increased to a canter as soon as their steeds' unshod hooves touched the springy surface of the velvet turf.

Two red lights blinked and shone from the ridge opposite. Above the riding column, the Guytrash watched and waited. The huge black dog had been tracking the Fairy Raid, keeping pace with them across the heath. This was his place. He had no quarrel with the Old Grey Man, but he had no love for the Lady, or any of her band. The Guytrash was a wily and canny hunter. He kept his great red eyes firmly on his quarry, the human child. He tensed now, judging the moment, his body taut and ready, his huge strength coiled back into his massive haunches. When the column split, he pounced.

17

Kate sat on the Whitestone. Tom said he'd seen figures up here on the hill. He'd thought it looked like a man on a horse, which could have been Jack. He'd thought he saw others close beside him, smaller, more childlike in size. One of them could have been Elizabeth. And the other? It could have been Davey. Kate had needed no more prompting. She'd run up and down the hills, forcing her way through gorse and briar and bracken. Her clothes were torn, she was covered in scratches, but when they got here, it had all been for nothing. There was no sign of anybody.

She wiped her eyes, smearing tears of bitter disappointment across the dirt on her face.

'People don't just disappear,' Elinor was saying. 'We ought to go back. Maybe he just went to bed, or something—'

'And maybe he didn't,' Kate glared up at her. 'And people *do* disappear. Don't you ever read the papers? Hundreds of them every year.'

'Yeah, but they aren't usually taken by fairies. There are rational explanations—'

'Oh, really? You've *seen* her, Ellie. She'd have taken that other little boy last year. He would have been a goner if Davey hadn't saved him.' Kate turned away as fresh tears started. 'Oh, how I wish, how I *wish* that we'd *listened* to him. He didn't want to go, remember?' Kate closed her eyes recalling last midsummer. 'If we'd listened to him, we never would have gone on that stupid ghost walk!'

'Yes, well, we did, didn't we?' Tom scuffed the grit at the side of the crossroads. 'There's no point in crying over it, and there's no point taking it out on Ellie. She's only trying to help.'

'I know,' Kate sniffed and wiped her nose on her sleeve. 'Sorry.'

'That's okay. Here—' Elinor offered her a tissue.

'Thanks.'

'No problem,' Elinor shrugged, hands in pockets. 'You keep it. I don't want it back.'

'What's that?' Something, a glint in the distance, had caught Tom's eye. He stood out in the crossroads, shading his eyes, gazing out to the west.

'What's what?'

'Over there,' Tom pointed. 'A red light. There it is again.'

Kate peered into the gathering darkness. 'Perhaps it's the sun, reflecting on something.'

'The sun's gone. Set.'

'Perhaps it's a car,' Elinor suggested.

'With red headlights?'

'Rear lights, then. You know, brake lights—'

Kate shook her head. 'There aren't any roads over

there.' She looked around. 'Everything looks different somehow, the Heath looks bigger . . . Perhaps it's a UFO,' she managed a lopsided grin. 'Seriously! There have been sightings out here. It's a whatd'yacallit? Hot spot. Or maybe it's those other things, earth lights—'

'Red lights, earth lights, UFO – whatever it is, it's weird,' Tom stared intensely. 'And weird is what we're looking for. Come on, let's go and see.'

18

The white pony whinnied, rolling its eyes in terror, as the huge dog leapt straight for it. Davey lost his grip on the reins as his mount shied, rearing on its hind legs. He fell backwards out of the saddle. The Guytrash was on him in the blink of an eye. The huge creature seized him in his massive jaws and began to drag him away from the milling confusion and up on to the opposite bank.

Fairy lances whistled past his gigantic head. A dart embedded itself in his shaggy neck. The Guytrash dropped his burden and turned, growling. Davey lay pale and crumpled between the paws of the great creature. Lisa thought he must be dead. The Guytrash moved forward, ready to meet his attackers, careful to put his enormous body between Davey and them. Lisa acted instinctively, without thought. In a second, she was out of her hiding-place, sprinting across the space in between. She knelt over Davey, feeling for his pulse, touching his face to see if he was still alive. His eyes were closed and he felt so cold. She took her green jacket off to cover him and put her arms round him to keep him warm.

'Lisa!' Elizabeth rose to go after her, but Jack held her back.

'Wait! We should not intervene.'

'How do you know?'

'I feel it is so. The Guytrash will not allow any harm to come to her. Perhaps it is meant.'

Elizabeth looked at the scene in front of her and whispered, 'I certainly hope you are right.'

The Guytrash was completely surrounded. His red eyes blazed and he continued to snarl his defiance. His tormentors danced out of the way of his scything paws and snapping jaws, jabbing at him with their leaf-bladed lances. They were aiming at his eyes, trying to blind him, while ranks of bowmen advanced upon him, short bows drawn to their deepest extent, ready to discharge their bolts deep into his flesh.

One word and he would be stuck like a pin-cushion. The Lady was standing in her stirrups, her emerald eyes, sparking cold fury, urging them on to the kill.

Suddenly a deep voice rang out like a bell.

'Hold!' The Old Grey Man ordered the circling warriors, his hand held high in command. 'I will not have the Old One harmed!' He pointed towards where the Guytrash stood at bay. The massive animal looked up, his huge lamp-like eyes glowing bright in recognition. 'He walked these hills before ever we came here.' The Old Grey Man twisted in his saddle to face his daughter. 'This thing has gone on too long. I say, enough! The choice has been made.' He pointed to where Davey lay, cradled in Lisa's arms. 'The Old One has saved the human child. One of his own has claimed him to herself.' He turned back to his

198

daughter. 'You must meddle no further. They have him fast.' The Lady stared over at the human boy whom she had coveted for so long. Her emerald eyes flared defiance, and her band looked to her, weapons drawn in readiness. Then she lowered her gaze. The Old Grey Man was both her father and her king. She was bound to him by blood and ealty – bonds that even she dare not break. 'It is settled then, daughter,' the Old Grey Man said, inclining his head, accepting her obedience. 'We will tarry here no longer. We have far to go this night. Come,' he wheeled his steed and pointed westward. 'We must away!'

The lancers and bowmen lowered their weapons and returned to their horses. The leading rider lifted a great green horn from his side and blew. A series of powerful notes belled through the gathering darkness. The Old Grey Man's call was taken in a general shout: 'Away! Away!'

The Old Grey Man spurred his horse and the whole column galloped after him headlong down the broad green path, and then they seemed to rise up, blackening the sky, blotting out the stars and the rising moon. The air was full of their wild high cries as they wheeled and turned, streaming off into the west like a great flock of migrating birds.

19

'They are gone.' Jack said, as he stepped from his hiding-place. 'He is safe. They will not return.'

Lisa looked up at him, her grey eyes all pupil. It was only now that she was beginning to realise exactly what she had done. Before it had been like a dream. Now she was waking up to find herself in the middle of the Heath, with a highwayman bending over her and Davey lying limp and still, half in her arms, half in her lap. She looked from him to the great shaggy bulk of the Guytrash sprawled close by and her eyes widened still further.

'Don't be alarmed,' Jack squeezed her shoulder. 'He will not harm you. See? He has pains of his own to deal with.'

The Guytrash was whining now, and licking himself, searching for hurts in his fur like any other dog.

'Come, Sir,' Jack addressed him formally. 'Let me look at you.'

The huge creature looked up, his red eyes dimmed by the wounds he had received. His enormous tongue unfurled from between long white teeth as sharp as knives and he licked Jack's hand. Then he shuffled over, awkwardly, on forelegs and haunches and licked Davey's face, as if his hot rough tongue could lick the life back into him.

It seemed to work. Under the rasping tongue, some of Davey's colour began to come back. He stirred and struggled, muttering to himself, as if in sleep. He was becoming too much for Lisa to hold. Elizabeth helped her to sit him up and between them they held him as he twisted and turned, wriggled and squirmed, became very hot and then very cold. Lisa wrapped her coat round him tighter. His eyes moved under the lids, his lips shaped words and he made sounds, although no sounds they could understand. It was as if he was vividly dreaming, and in the dream he was transforming, changing from one shape into another.

All they could do was hold him. Jack looked at him closely, peeling his eyelid back. The eyeball moved, scanning some inner world that only he could see.

'At least he's still alive, and not with *them*,' Jack said.

'Will he come out of it?' Lisa asked.

'I don't know. Keep him warm. Hold him tight while I tend to the Guytrash.'

Jack searched through the twisted cables of the creature's thick fur, looking for elf bolts, the short-shafted lethal darts that the Fair Folk had discharged. The Guytrash lay obedient, head on paws, hardly flinching. Only the odd twitch of the skin or lift of the head showed the pain he was suffering. Jack lined the arrows up in a row. Luckily none of them had penetrated very deeply. Most of the wounds were superficial. The important thing was to get them all out. They were cunningly made. He turned one between finger and thumb, admiring the elegant feathered flights and finely knapped razor-sharp blades. They were set about with spells besides. Any left beneath the skin would cause the flesh to fester, and might even work their way deep inside and through to his heart. He looked at the white streak left by an old wound in the big dog's black flank. This was the second time that he had saved the Guytrash.

When he had finished, Jack wiped his hands on the grass and came to see how Davey was doing.

'He's quieter now,' Lisa said. 'But he shows no signs of coming out of it.' She bit her lip. 'Perhaps we should get him to a doctor . . .'

Jack laughed out loud. 'Leeches have no cure for what ails this boy. Lay him next to the Guytrash. They can warm each other.'

Lisa was not sure, but she did as she was told. The great dog turned his head, the light showing red from under the lids. He nosed Davey as though the boy was a puppy and began to lick him again. The big tongue was warm and wet, and as rough as sandpaper. This time Davey did more than stir. He put his hand up to his face.

'Ugh! Get off me!' He opened his eyes to see what it was, his features twisted in a grimace of disgust.

'Davey!' Lisa put her arms round him, hugging him to her.

'You can get off, too,' Davey struggled to escape her embrace, thinking it was Kate. Then his deep brown eyes widened as he saw who it was. 'Lisa? What are you doing? What is the matter with you?'

She held his chin, looking deep into his eyes.

'They're brown! They're brown! Oh, Davey!' She grinned at him. 'I could kiss you!'

'Well, don't,' Davey edged away. 'Of course they're brown. What colour do you think they'd be?' He edged away a bit farther, in case Lisa had turned into a crazy person.

'It's all right, Davey.' Elizabeth smiled down at him. 'We're not insane. Just glad to have you back.'

'Where have I been?' Davey looked around. 'What am I doing here? What's been happening?'

'It's a long story—'

'Is that Jack? And the Guytrash?' The great dog was lumbering to its feet. 'Is that what licked me?' Davey put his hand to his face again. 'No wonder it felt like I was trapped in a car wash.'

Davey really was back. His eyes were their normal deep brown. He sat up, Lisa's jacket falling from him. Even the strange shimmering clothes he'd worn had changed back to the jeans and T-shirt he'd been wearing when he left the house. He looked around. They were on the Heath somewhere, he could work that much out, but why, and how he had got there, he had no idea.

The Guytrash stood up slowly, staggering slightly, then shook himself, the movement rippling from nose to tail, like a dog shaking off water. He moved his big head from side to side, looking from one to the other, then he raised his nose, as though he had caught another scent in the air, something new and interesting. It was time for him to go. He gave a whine, as if in farewell. Jack bowed and wished him goodnight. He knew better than to thank him for his help.

'We must leave, too,' he said after the Guytrash had gone. 'We must return to the city or Polly will worry. At dawn we depart. We must be back long before that.'

'Depart?' Davey looked up, puzzled and concerned. 'Where to? Where are you going?'

'We are leaving the city. All the ghosts.'

'Polly and Govan? The Fiddler, too?'

'All.'

'Forever?'

'Yes,' Jack said quietly, bowing his head.

Oh, no . . .' Davey said.

Jack, Elizabeth, Polly, Govan and the Fiddler might be ghosts, but they were his friends. At the thought of losing them, of never ever seeing them again, Davey's heart seemed to swell painfully in his chest. It was like the feeling rushing back into a limb after some extended paralysis. First came pins and needles, then shooting agonising pain. Davey winced and his eyes filled. He sat where he was. The feeling was so intense it was physical.

'It is time for us to go,' Elizabeth knelt down beside him, putting her arm round him. 'Thanks to you, the

Judge and the Sentinels rule no longer. The Book of Possibilities is closed. What Was, and What Is, have become What *Has* to Be.'

'I understand, I do,' Davey blinked the tears back. 'It's just . . .'

'Do you not think we feel the same way, too?' Elizabeth squeezed his shoulder. 'We will miss you, but we must leave now. We must. To everything there is a time, and our time has come.'

'I know,' Davey sniffed. It was like coming home from a bitter wind-blown frozen wilderness only to find that all your friends were leaving.

'We will meet again. Some day you, too, will go through the Door of No Returning.'

'Where does it lead?'

'To the other side.'

'What is it like?'

'We don't know,' Elizabeth stared away into the darkness. 'No one ever comes back. One day you will find out.' Her mouth curled in a smile, but her eyes stayed sad. 'But not for a good long while I hope.'

Davey looked at her and saw a girl who was younger than he was now. Their eyes met, and hers seemed suddenly full of tears, but whether she cried for him, or for what might have been, he just couldn't tell.

'Ghosts don't cry,' she said, smiling again as Davey took a handkerchief from his pocket.

'Elizabeth,' Jack was calling her. 'Time runs on.'

'I must go,' she reached over and kissed him lightly. Her lips felt cool and soft on his cheek.

'Go safely, Elizabeth,' he whispered.

'Stay well, Davey.'

20

Jack did not like goodbyes.

'Come, Elizabeth. We have far to travel,' he said, helping her up into the saddle. 'And you,' he turned to Davey, his dark handsome face serious and sad for a moment. Then he smiled and his black eyes gleamed with unexpected tenderness. He tapped the boy gently on the side of his face, two gloved fingers tipping his chin. 'You stay away from trouble.'

Then he was mounted. He saluted once from the back of his horse, waving his hat in farewell, and he was gone. Davey sank back to the ground buried his head in his hands, and cried.

'Never mind, Davey, never mind,' Lisa said, putting her arm round him. 'It's probably for the best. They *have* to go. You heard what they said.'

'I know, it's just . . .' Davey's muffled voice came back.

'Have a good cry,' she patted his back. 'Does you good sometimes, that's what my gran says.'

Especially after what happened to you, she thought, but she didn't tell him that. His tears were cleansing, healing, washing away the poison inside him, replacing it with human feeling.

'We'd better think about getting back ourselves,' she

said, after he seemed to have cried himself out. 'Mum will be wondering where I am.'

She didn't want to alarm anybody, but that was probably a bit of an understatement. It was a wonder search and rescue helicopters weren't circling right this second.

'Can you walk okay?' she asked as she helped him to his feet.

'Yeah, I'll be fine,' he leaned on her shoulder. 'Just give me a minute.'

They had been sitting down in between thickets of bracken and gorse. As soon as they stood up, they became visible. They rose, almost at Tom's feet, as unexpected as a couple of pheasant. He jumped back in surprise from where he'd been standing, staring around, wondering where else to look. The source of his red lights had long ago melted away into the night.

'Hey, Ellie, Kate, over here!' Tom shouted, waving to his sister and cousin. 'Where did you two spring from?'

'Nowhere. We've been here all the time . . .'

'We've been looking everywhere. Are you all right?' He looked at Davey. 'Kate's been ever so worried.'

'Yeah, I'm okay,' Davey started to say, but just then Kate came running over.

'Lisa! What are you doing here? Are you all right?' She turned to her brother. Her intense relief at finding him again melting into concern at the shake in his voice, the whiteness of his face. She began looking in his eyes like a doctor.

'I'm fine, Kate,' Davey struggled out of her grip. 'Get off me!'

'He seems okay,' Lisa intervened. She was afraid that Kate's fretting might be too much for Davey's newly-hatched feelings. 'Has anyone got a watch?' She asked, deliberately changing the subject. 'I left mine at home, but I think it's late.' She looked at Tom's wrist and went pale. 'I'd better go. My mum'll kill me.'

'Here,' Kate handed her the mobile phone. 'Ring her on this. Say you're at our house.'

'But it's only just round the corner,' Lisa punched in the number. 'She'll want me back – like – now.'

'Say you're staying over.'

'Thanks, Kate. That's a great idea.'

As soon as Lisa finished her call, the phone rang. It was Alison Williams wanting to know why there was no one at home.

'Hi, Mum.' Kate replied. 'We're round at Lisa's house—

'—Lisa Wilson, Davey's friend—

'—All of us. Yeah. Playing a game—

'—Kind of a war thing, involving fairies and elves and stuff—

'—Soon, yeah. I *know* she *only lives* round the corner—

'—Okay, okay. Oh, Mum – can Lisa stay the night—?

'—Well, because . . .

'—I know, but she wants to—

'—She can sleep in Emma's room—

'—Great! Thanks, Mum!

'—Yeah. See you later.

'That's all sorted then.' Kate returned the phone to her inside pocket. 'Let's go home.'

It was strange. Each of them thought the village was a long, long way from this place on the Heath, and that it would take them ages to reach it. But that wasn't the case. In what seemed like no time, they were in amongst familiar surroundings, walking on the pavement of their own estate. They all knew that time could shift, and with it space, so perhaps Wesson Heath itself had changed, shrinking back from a wild expanse to its present day, more user-friendly size. Either that, or maybe the way back is always shorter, an easier distance to make than the outward journey into places unknown.

21

They travelled quickly, the way it is in dreams. One second you are in one place, the next you are in quite another. Davey, Kate, Tom, Elinor and Lisa. They looked at each other and knew that they were dreaming the same thing, at the same time, which was an impossible thing. They were dreaming all together.

They were in a high place looking out over the river. They were here to see their friends. They were here to say goodbye.

At the very edge of the cliff stood the high wall, the curtain of stone, fretted like lace with arches and windows. The central archway was tall and pointed like an arrow head. This was the Door of No Returning. The time was midsummer dawning. It was time for the ghosts to pass through.

Their friends were there and waiting for them. Jack and Polly stood together, their hands loosely linked. Elizabeth and Govan stood either side of the Blind Fiddler, who no longer carried a staff, his hands resting on their shoulders. The children approached, their dream tread as silent as a ghost walking. Their friends heard them, and smiled in greeting, but their eyes were already fixed on the far horizon.

The cliff faced east. Across the river, the sky was beginning to lighten from indigo to deep cobalt. As the children watched, the first point of light pricked the dark intense blue. Rays radiated out into a luminous halo, filling the Door of No Returning, turning the short springy grass to vibrant greenness, touching the big squat boulder in the centre, making it taller, thinner, casting a shadow like a finger pointing straight towards them.

The Door of No Returning spilled whiteness. The time for leaving was fast approaching. Wave after wave of black shapes showed against the blazing light. On the very brink of departure, their ghost friends turned to smile again and even the dawn's brilliance could not match the radiance on their faces. There could be no more sadness, all sense of sorrow was wiped away.

Davey was convinced of the rightness of things, as one by one, the ghosts left, passing like shadows, to be lost in the dazzling brightness of the sun's new day.

h HODDER *Another Hodder Children's Book*

CITY OF SHADOWS

Celia Rees

The start of a compelling trilogy

All through the city and its suburbs, the past lies behind the present and ghosts shadow the living. There are threshold zones, borderlines, and places where the laws of time and space falter. Strange things can happen, the barriers between the worlds grow thin and it is possible, just possible, to move from world to another . . .

It is the summer of his twelfth birthday, and Davey, his sister Kate and his twin cousins, join the hoards of tourists eager to catch a glimpse of the legendary Underground city in Davey's hometown. A harmless trip. Just a bit of fun. But for Davey it is the start of a nightmare, and a long, terrifying battle with the dead . . .

A TRAP IN TIME

Celia Rees

Part two of the chilling trilogy that began with *City of Shadows*

All through the city and its suburbs, the past lies behind the present and ghosts shadow the living. There are threshold zones, borderlines, and places where the laws of time and space falter. Strange things can happen, the barriers between the worlds grow thin and it is possible, just possible, to move from world to another . . .

Davey had hoped that the chilling events of Midsummer and Halloween were all part of a terrible dream – a dream he never wants to have again. But Christmas brings a new horror: Davey's archenemy, the Lady, is back to get revenge . . . and an archaeological dig uncovers more than just an old building. For Davey, Elinor, Kate and Tom, it unleashes a terrifying and unearthly force, which they will need all their strength, and Davey's gift for Second Sight, to resist . . .